Charlie felt just a stirring of interest. Was Karen experiencing the same thing? The suggestion that they'd missed something important as kids and that it was more than fate that they were both back in Bramble Bay?

"About the prom," she said, still holding his hand.

"Yes?"

"I thought you were asking me as some kind of dare. You were a senior after all, and I was a lowly sophomore. You were popular and I was...me."

"There was no dare," Charlie assured her.

She looked mystified. "I couldn't believe you wanted to date *me*. I thought it had to be some ploy to see if you could..."

"Seduce you," he finished for her. "That was the word you used then. And since it wasn't even what I'd had in mind, it took me a while to figure out what you were talking about."

"I thought it was on everybody's mind."

"Was it on your mind?"

She blushed instantly

"Well, I'll be..."

Welcome, newest eHarlequin.com member!

As you know, when it comes to romance, no one compares to Harlequin. When it comes to romance online, eHarlequin.com is unequivocally the best Internet destination for romantic escape. These 2 FREE books have been written exclusively for eHarlequin.com and are available only from www.eHarlequin.com. They are our way of saying welcome to romance online!

Be sure to explore all of www.eHarlequin.com. The site is divided into three main channels:

❤ **Your Romantic Books** is the place to read, write and shop. You can purchase Harlequin, Silhouette, MIRA and Steeple Hill books at great discounts. Read online romance serials, find fascinating information about all your favorite authors, and meet them in our message boards.

❤ **Your Romantic Life** features expert advice on romance and relationships, and how-to guides for making your love life richer and more exciting. Included are features such as: Recipes for Romance; Dr. Romance—our romance expert who answers a new relationship question each week; and Virtual Hints—which lets you send a virtual hint to your sweetheart reminding him of an upcoming special event!

❤ **Your Romantic Escapes** promises to be the ultimate in online indulgence, featuring lovescopes that forecast love and passion for you, romantic travel destinations, romantic movie reviews and interactive games, such as Six Degrees of On-Screen Kisses—a fun celebrity kissing game.

I'm sure you'll enjoy every minute of the time you spend on www.eHarlequin.com. We aim to satisfy all your online romance desires.

Happy reading!

Brian E. Hickey

Brian E. Hickey
President, eHarlequin.com
Chairman, Harlequin Enterprises Limited

MURIEL JENSEN

Home To You

HARLEQUIN®

TORONTO • NEW YORK • LONDON
AMSTERDAM • PARIS • SYDNEY • HAMBURG
STOCKHOLM • ATHENS • TOKYO • MILAN • MADRID
PRAGUE • WARSAW • BUDAPEST • AUCKLAND

ISBN 0-373-15327-9

HOME TO YOU

Copyright © 2000 by Muriel Jensen.

All rights reserved. Except for use in any review, the reproduction or
utilization of this work in whole or in part in any form by any electronic,
mechanical or other means, now known or hereafter invented, including
xerography, photocopying and recording, or in any information storage
or retrieval system, is forbidden without the written permission of the
publisher, Harlequin Enterprises Limited, 225 Duncan Mill Road,
Don Mills, Ontario, Canada M3B 3K9.

All characters in this book have no existence outside the imagination of
the author and have no relation whatsoever to anyone bearing the same
name or names. They are not even distantly inspired by any individual
known or unknown to the author, and all incidents are pure invention.

This edition published by arrangement with Harlequin Books S.A.

® and TM are trademarks of the publisher. Trademarks indicated with
® are registered in the United States Patent and Trademark Office, the
Canadian Trade Marks Office and in other countries.

Visit us at www.eHarlequin.com

Printed in U.S.A.

Dear Reader,

I am delighted to know that I've come *Home To You* as a special gift from eHarlequin.com. The best part about the Internet to me is the ease and immediacy of author-reader contact.

What a boon for all of us that we can now shop and order books online. Like you, I'm always in pursuit of my favorite writer's latest book. Even if it isn't yet available, there's something comforting about being able to view the cover and know the date of its availability. Having it delivered to my home isn't bad, either!

Which brings me to *Home To You*. "Home" is something we all understand—either because we have it and know that it enriches us, or because we long for it and know we'll never be complete without it.

And the remarkable thing is that "home" doesn't have to have been a perfect experience to give us our richest memories. Most often we remember the quarrels, the struggles and the compromises the most vividly, and I think the knowledge that we endured and prevailed is what equips us for life.

My heroine in *Home To You* finally comes to understand that when she returns home after a long absence. She also learned that home can sometimes be found in the right man's arms.

My best to all of you for much love and laughter.

Muriel Jensen

To Ron—
who makes anywhere home for me.

CHAPTER ONE

KAREN TILLMAN STOOD in the middle of the living room of her grandmother's Victorian home, trying to accept that it now belonged to her. The paperwork said so. Someone, probably her mother, had repainted the name on the mailbox. And the fuel oil bill that had been hanging on the doorknob when she walked in was in her name.

In practical Judith Folker Tillman fashion, her grandmother had paid the Sunny Seniors Residence Resort in Florida three years in advance for her lodging when a recent broken arm at age eighty-four made it difficult for her to live alone. She gave her stocks and bonds to Karen's brother Peter, and her jewelry to his twin, Paula.

"The house," she'd told Karen when Karen came to visit her before she left, "is for you. You're the one who loved my tea parties and my candlelight dinners."

Tea and dinner had been her grandmother's attempts to force a little style and good manners into her wild grandchildren.

"But, Grandma," Karen had argued. "You're going to make it to your ninetieth birthday. You should keep the house until then and you can sell it if you have to support the rest of your—"

"I won't be able to stand my sister or my arthritis

for more than three years," Judith had interrupted. Her sister Ruth lived at the same retirement home. "They can put me on an ice floe and push me out to sea. I don't want to suffer with these aches and pains any longer than that."

"There are no ice floes in Florida." Karen had tried to match her imperious tone. "And the warm weather will make you forget you have arthritis."

But gentle by nature, she was no match for her querulous grandmother. "I was being metaphorical, dear. Some Native American tribes simply put their old people beyond the protection of the camp and let nature take its course."

"Yes, well in your case that would be you casting a flirtatious eye in the direction of the first well-heeled gentleman to walk by, then spending your declining years with him on weekly senior tours to Vegas or the Jersey shore." Her grandmother's love of community Bingo games, and casino slot machines was well known.

Judith had laughed. "Then what are you worried about? I'll be fine. And you should come home to Bramble Bay now that you managed to get your heart broken as well as your bank account."

Karen had closed her eyes and let that brutal assessment of her situation roll off her back. It was the only way to deal with her father's mother.

"Mr. Finnegan's at some geezer farm in Florida now, too, you know," her grandmother had added. "I'm going to find him when I get there."

The conversation had turned to a discussion of Judith's sometimes boyfriend, and by the time the conversation was over, Karen was informed that her grandmother's attorney would handle all the paperwork involved in the transfer of ownership of the house.

The more Karen thought about it as she took a week to sell her apartment and office furniture in Seattle, Washington, the more taking over the big old house seemed like a good idea—at least temporarily. She had to make a living, and she couldn't go into competition with her father in the accounting business. And she could never work *for* him because his obsession with detail would drive her insane.

But she could turn Blackberry House into a bed-and-breakfast. She'd had three B-&-B owners among her clients, and though she'd seen two of them fail, she had confidence that conditions were very different in Bramble Bay than they were in Portland.

Firstly, there were only two other bed-and-breakfasts in town at the moment, and Blackberry House had a view of the water the other two couldn't match. The original builder of the house had so named it because of the tenacious wild blackberries from which he was always trying to reclaim the garden. Those same prickly berries had also given the town its name.

Secondly, the house was perfectly situated on a knoll overlooking the half-moon-shaped bay, was only four blocks from downtown, and the next lot was occupied by Porter's Galley, the finest restaurant in the county.

For the first time in the six weeks since she'd stood at the automatic bank machine, watched it eat her bankcard, and flash the warning Account Closed, Karen felt a glimmer of enthusiasm.

It had flickered bravely for most of the four-hour drive home. It died abruptly when she faced the truth that everyone in town had probably read the headline in the *Oregonian,* Con Artist Bilks Fiancée Out of Savings and Assets. And then when Brian had been caught a week later in Monte Carlo, the simple: All is Lost for Portland CPA said it all.

Brian Spencer, whom she'd met at a conference of northwest CPAs, and eventually invited into her business and her life, had spent half a million dollars in gambling and high living on the Riviera. Everything he'd stolen from her was gone.

She paid her employees their last month's wages, and repaid the trust account that held her clients' estimated tax payments with her Gold Card. Now she owed her credit card her firstborn child.

So, she told herself philosophically, walking through the large living room furnished in old brocade and dark wood, there were worse things than public humiliation. She just couldn't think of what they were.

She flipped on the light in the big country kitchen. Her grandmother had had the room updated and the bedrooms painted just two years ago. She went to the glass-fronted cupboards that showed off her grandmother's gold-trimmed Limoges china and the backsplash in hand-painted tiles in green, burgundy and gold.

She remembered her grandmother boasting that the carpenter she'd hired did fine woodworking and that he'd helped her keep the renovation true to the house's Victorian style.

Karen took several steps back, studying the open flow from the living room into the kitchen. She'd seen the new kitchen when she'd come home for Christmas last year, and though she'd loved it, she thought it needed something to block the view of a messy counter or uncleared kitchen table.

The grapevine carvings on the cupboards made her wonder how a half counter would look, perhaps with some decorative trim.

She realized with the force of exhaustion that she was just too tired to think about it now. She'd lain awake for weeks, wondering what to do about her financial problems; she'd been packing and selling things off for days, and she'd driven almost two hundred miles today. She needed sleep.

She headed for the front door and her car, determined to find her overnight bag that contained her nightgown, her toothbrush and her makeup. The rest of the bags and boxes could wait until tomorrow. She wanted a hot shower and the crown-topped bed in the front bedroom with the sheer draperies surrounding it.

She flipped on the porch light but nothing happened. Making a mental note to check the bulb in the morning, she opened the door, stepped out onto the porch thinking that dusk had fallen quickly, caught her toe on something that screeched, and fell flat on her face.

Stunned, she lay still for a moment, trying to assess what had happened, and whether or not she'd broken anything. A multiple fracture was just what her current situation needed for added drama.

Somewhere in an unfocused corner of her mind she heard a child's cry, a man's oath, and the sound of water lapping in the bay.

Then she was turned over by a pair of strong hands and her upper body lifted and rested against something solid—a braced knee? The shadows were too deep for her to see much at first glance.

She felt fingertips brush the hair out of her face and a voice that struck a familiar chord said, "Karen?"

She was very close to a man's face, his arms wrapped around her so that the entire world in that instant seemed composed of soft fleece and the subtle fragrance of a spicy aftershave. She struggled to identify the voice.

"Maybe she's dead!" a young, high voice said with more anticipation than she would have liked associated with that possibility.

"She's not dead," the man said patiently. "She just fell over something."

"She kicked Hannibal," the child replied. "He ran away."

"Karen." A hand caught her chin in the V of thumb and forefinger and turned her toward the face. "Say something. Are you hurt?"

Her eyes finally adjusting to the shadows, Karen looked up into a man's pleasant, angular face with a strong nose and watchful eyes. His hair was straight, several strands springing up from a precise side part and falling onto his forehead.

Though she couldn't determine the color of his hair and eyes in the shadows, sudden recognition struck her and she jolted a little in his arms, trying to sit up.

"Charlie Scott!" she said in astonishment.

He held fast, grinning. "Right. Apparently you didn't hit your head. Does anything hurt?" His hands ran gently along her arms, as though testing for injury. "Judith won't be very pleased if you end up in traction your first day home."

Karen lay still as his hands came to rest at her waist. Her adolescent fantasies had been composed of just this scenario, only in her dreams they'd been married and his hands had wandered everywhere.

In those days Charlie Scott had been her brother's friend, a football star, president or chairman of every club or function at Bramble Bay High School in his senior year, and she'd been brainy Karen Tillman, a little plain, a little awkward, and very defensive about following in the footsteps of her beautiful and brilliant twin siblings, Peter and Paula, Charlie's classmates.

At that age of hormonal turmoil, she'd imagined herself superior to the struggles of those around her, responding to their confusion over her behavior with what she considered biting wit.

Though she chided her friends for lusting after the handsome and powerful senior boys, she'd had a secret crush on Charlie Scott. She'd imagined their lives together.

In her dreams, she created children for them—a girl named Charlen, the combination of their two names, and a boy named Raymond James after their two fathers.

She had indulged her fantasy to intricate detail, then one day reality fell on her like space debris when he stopped her just outside of the cafeteria and asked her to the senior prom.

She groaned now as she remembered how she'd responded to that invitation with horrid rudeness.

"Does that mean something does hurt?" Charlie asked her now.

"No," she replied, finally finding her voice and realizing that he probably didn't even remember that fourteen-year-old exchange. "It means that I'm fine, but embarrassed. What happened?"

He braced her weight with an arm around her and helped her to her feet. "Your grandmother feeds a stray on the front porch. He probably saw you and thought she was home. He's all black, so you wouldn't have seen him in the shadows."

"There he is!" A boy about six dressed in jeans and a red fleece jacket picked up a large black cat off the porch railing. The cat had a flat face and a large plumy tail that suggested Persian ancestry.

"Judith named him Hannibal," the boy said, bringing the cat close enough for Karen to pet. "'Cause he likes to sit on her elephant table." He pointed to the natural wicker table shaped like an elephant. It sat between two wicker chairs with pink-and-green cushions.

Karen stroked the large head cautiously. The cat allowed it, then jumped out of the boy's arms and went to an empty Blue Willow bowl near a potted pink geranium. Karen recognized a dessert bowl from the many childhood tea parties.

"I can show you where she keeps the cat food," the boy volunteered.

"Ah...sure."

The boy bolted through the open doorway into the house.

Charlie pointed after him. "My son, Ben," he said, reaching for the porch light switch.

Karen felt a small and inexplicable twinge of pain. No Charlen. No Raymond James. But another woman's Ben. Those long-ago dreams about Charlie just weren't meant to be.

"Bulb must be out." She went inside, thinking that that seemed to be the case about most of her dreams lately. Not meant to be. Bulb burned out. But that was all right. She'd made up her mind that she was lucky to have been able to pay what she could of the debt Brian had left, and all she had to do now was support herself until she could pay off her credit card and figure out what she really wanted to do with the rest of her life.

The bed-and-breakfast was a stop-gap measure, but she was lucky to have it.

When Karen and Charlie caught up to Ben in the kitchen, he was delving into a cabinet under the counter. He emerged with a little flat can and held it up triumphantly. "He likes liver and chicken the best." He contorted his beautiful little face. He had pink cheeks, light blue eyes, one scalloped bud of a permanent front tooth and a space where its companion should be. "It really stinks, but he doesn't care. Want me to put it in his bowl?"

Karen nodded. "Yes, please."

Ben opened a drawer, pulled out a teaspoon, and ran out to the front porch.

And left Karen alone with Charlie Scott.

CHARLIE WAS NOT SURPRISED that bratty Karen Tillman had grown into a beautiful woman. Toward the end of his senior year, he'd just begun to see her potential. She'd grown several inches, developed a small but pronounced chest, and was acquiring an air of femininity about her that was special. And she'd been smarter than most of the girls he knew, and not afraid to show it.

Now she was five feet six or seven in a pair of tennis shoes, a good two-thirds of her height filling faded jeans with slender and shapely curves. Breasts a little fuller than he remembered were defined by a simple, round-necked red sweater. Glossy dark brown hair was caught high on her head in a fat, curly ponytail.

In her large brown eyes he saw the same haughty wit with which she'd often bludgeoned him and his friends in high school. He'd never understood then what he'd done to deserve her abuse, but her brother had explained to him that she treated everyone that way.

Then he'd found himself on a Spanish Club fund-raising committee with her and he'd seen a smart, hardworking, resourceful side of her he'd had to admire. She'd behaved so differently from the other girls who pursued him with flattering but tiresome determination, that he wanted to know her better. So he'd asked her to the prom.

She'd refused him harshly, accusing him of cruel teasing and telling him in no uncertain terms what she thought of him. He'd been so shocked and offended, he hadn't asked again.

She closed the cupboard door Ben had left open and leaned against the counter, smiling at him with cool politeness.

"How is it that you and your son know my grandmother's house so well?" she asked.

He thought the unspoken suggestion was that she didn't like that fact.

"I did a lot of work for her," he replied. "In fact,

she gave me a key. Ben and I have been feeding Hannibal since Judith went to Florida. I saw your light on and was coming to return the key to you.'' He dug it out of his pants pocket and handed it to her, happy to display the evidence that her grandmother had trusted him, even if she didn't.

She accepted it and studied him with a frown. ''I thought you were going into journalism. I seem to remember Peter telling me you were in Lebanon.''

''I did. I was.'' He didn't want to say more on the subject, but his reply seemed to simply hang there, unjustified. ''My priorities changed,'' he added.

She nodded, angling her chin toward the door. ''Ben?''

''Yes.''

''Handsome little boy.''

''Yes.''

He saw the obvious question in her eyes.

''His mother died in China,'' he said briefly. ''She was a reporter, too.''

''I'm sorry.'' She looked first horrified, then sincere. ''How long have you been back home?''

''Since Ben was born.''

''July 19!'' Ben said as he raced back into the room. ''How come you're talking about my birthday? Didn't I already have it?''

Charlie nodded, looking into his son's bright eyes and thinking how his first glimpse into them had changed his entire life. ''Yes, you did. It's not coming around for another eight-and-a-half months. So don't start making a gift list or anything.''

Ben came to stand beside him and hook his hand into the crook of Charlie's arm. ''But it's almost time to make a Christmas list, isn't it?''

Charlie laughed and ruffled his hair. "Always angling, aren't you? Yes it is. But you have a little time yet."

"When's it going to be Halloween?"

"A couple of weeks."

Ben smiled winningly at Karen. "Can I come here to trick-or-treat?"

She smiled at him. Charlie liked the look in her eyes when they rested on Ben. It showed a basic love of children. Anyone's children. "Of course you can. What's your favorite kind of candy?"

"Peanut butter cups," Ben replied. "I'm going to be something great! Only I don't know what. Do you have kids?"

"Nope." She looked regretful. Charlie wondered if it was genuine, or just intended to embellish her reply for Ben's sake. "No kids."

Ben looked around. "Won't you be scared all by yourself?"

"I won't be all by myself too long. After Christmas, this is going to be a bed-and-breakfast. Do you know what that is?"

"Like a hotel?"

"Right. So I'll have people around all the time."

"But you'll be all alone until Christmas."

"I have to have a few repairs made," she explained patiently. "And a few things built."

Ben smiled and turned to Charlie. "That's what my dad does. Builds things."

Karen cast an uncomfortable glance at Charlie then smiled apologetically at Ben. "I'm going to hire the same carpenter my grandmother used because he—"

Charlie remained silent, hands in his pockets as

their conversation went on, knowing just where this was going and liking it.

"That's my dad," Ben interrupted. "Bay Carpentry. That's Dad."

Charlie really liked her astonishment.

She pointed to the grape motif on the cabinetry. "You did that?"

He nodded modestly. "I did."

After a moment of surprised silence, she smiled dryly at him. "That's quite a skill for a *second* career choice."

"I work hard at it," he said. "What did you want done?"

She went to the spot where the kitchen met the living room. When Charlie followed her, Ben occupied himself by playing a hybrid game of hopscotch, leaping from one floor tile to another, ignoring the adult discussion.

Karen spread her arms to indicate the area from the edge of the kitchen counter to about halfway across to the other side. "I was thinking about a room divider here," she explained. "Something that would separate the rooms without blocking off the light. Maybe a counter with a decorative finish on this side and drawers or shelves on the kitchen side. I love the old living room and I love the new kitchen, so I don't want to spoil either, but I thought a little divider between the two so you can't see mess in the kitchen from the living room."

"Good idea."

She cleared her throat. "Would you...have time in the next few months?"

"I'll check my schedule. I think I have a few things that can wait."

"Do you need a deposit of some kind?"

Like everyone else who read a paper or listened to the news, he knew about everything she'd lost in the past few months.

"No." He smiled. "Just a 'You're hired' will do it."

"All right, then." She met his eyes and offered her hand. "You're hired."

He took it. It felt very small in his. "Thank you. I'll be back in a couple of days with some suggestions." He tried to withdraw his hand, but she retained her grip on it, a small pleat between her eyebrows.

He felt just a stirring of sexual interest. Was she experiencing the same thing he felt? The suggestion that they'd missed something important as kids and that it was more than fate that they were both back in Bramble Bay?

"About the prom," she said, still holding his hand.

"Yes?"

She tried several times to speak, then finally sighed and dropped her hand. "It's usually hard for me to admit to being a jerk," she said finally, "but I've had a lot of experience lately. I thought you were asking me as some kind of dare. You were a senior after all, and I was a lowly sophomore. You were popular and I was...me. So I climbed all over you."

He'd been hurt and confused over her refusal at the time, but had hardly thought about it since until Judith told him she was coming home.

"There was no dare," he assured her, "unless you consider that I dared myself. I found you interesting, and you *were* just a little underclassman with a lot of mouth and not much else to recommend you.'' He blunted that merciless assessment with a smile. ''And I did make sure none of the guys knew you'd turned me down.''

She looked mystified. ''You had cheerleaders after you. Barbie Warwick, for heaven's sake. I couldn't believe you wanted to date *me*. I thought it had to be some ploy to see if you could...'' She paused, clearly groping for the right word.

''Seduce you,'' he finished for her. ''That was the word you used. I remember because kids never use it to describe having sex. And since it wasn't even what I had in mind, it took me a minute to figure out what you were talking about.''

She shrugged a shoulder in what seemed to be embarrassment. ''I thought it was on everybody's mind.''

He looked into her eyes, watched her gaze hold his then slip away, and caught a glimpse of something he hadn't been wise enough to see at seventeen.

''Was it on *your* mind?'' he asked.

She blushed instantly, furiously.

He felt a strange, unexpected, long overdue sense of triumph. ''Well, I'll be damned,'' he muttered. She'd wanted *him*.

''Do *not* gloat,'' she warned him.

He made a point of keeping a sober face. ''I wouldn't think of it,'' he said gravely.

''You were the quarterback,'' she said, apparently feeling the need to defend herself. Her voice rose a little. ''The jock, the hunk all the other girls were after. It was just a silly, teenage...thing. And I got over it. So, there's no need for either of us to be embarrassed.''

"I'm not embarrassed."

She studied him suspiciously. "I don't want you to have any concerns about working here."

"I have none."

She drew a breath and angled her chin. "And I don't want you to think this…makes me in any way vulnerable."

"Aren't we all vulnerable?" he asked gently.

"I'm not," she replied firmly. "Not anymore. So, if you have any lingering interest in me after all this time, the safe thing would be to forget it."

HE'D BEEN GENTLEMANLY and considerate of her feelings throughout this uncomfortable discussion, but Karen saw something suddenly shift in his eyes at her suggestion.

"Is that required if I work here?" he asked, holding her gaze.

She wasn't sure she understood the question. "What do you mean?"

"I was a foreign correspondent," he said, his gaze steady. "I covered Afghanistan, Lebanon, Romania, Mogadishu. It's not in my nature to do the safe thing."

She was both flattered and alarmed by the suggestion that he *was* still interested.

"You came home to Bramble Bay," she pointed out.

"That was the right thing," he corrected. "Not the safe thing."

All right. She had to clarify this once and for all.

"I have no interest whatsoever in even attempting a relationship at this time."

"You've made that clear." He shifted his weight. "But I think I'm even more interested now than I was fourteen years ago. Do you want me around under those conditions?"

While she sputtered for an answer, astonished by his insistence, he added, "Bearing in mind that I go to your church, deliver your firewood, have dinner at your brother's house every couple of weeks. So, it's not like you'd never have to see me anyway."

She took a final stand to turn him off. "Are you threatening me with harassment?" she demanded.

He covered the small distance between them and stopped within an inch of her. "No," he replied softly, smiling. "I'm threatening you with a bona fide, dyed-in-the-wool, old-fashioned courtship. Can you take it?"

"You've read what happened to me," she reminded him. "I think I'll be immune to masculine charms for a good long time."

He grinned. "I've already waited fourteen years. Am I still hired?"

"Charlie—"

"Am I?"

She thought about the desperate need to get her life together, to make it appear to her already together parents and siblings that she could do *something* without disastrous results, and that she had to get this house on its feet as a bed-and-breakfast to accomplish that. And that she needed some special carpentry done to make that happen.

She hoped she knew what she was doing. "You're hired," she said.

"Good." He smiled. "See you in a couple of days with some plans. Come on, Ben. Gotta go."

Karen followed Charlie and his son to the door, then waved as Ben turned at the door of a large red truck and called a goodbye. Then the truck drove away with the roar of a powerful motor.

Karen couldn't dispel the feeling that it had run her over before it pulled away.

CHAPTER TWO

KAREN HAD ALWAYS LOVED the bed with the draperies falling from a large wooden crown on the ceiling. When she and the twins stayed overnight with their grandmother, she'd let the girls sleep in it. Peter had preferred the room with the ship's bed.

She lay in the middle of it now, the sheer curtains draped around the bed, sheened by moonlight from the window, and thought with a little twinge of regret how alone she felt in it. As a child, she'd thought how nice it would be to have the bed to herself, without Paula, who tended to sleep diagonally, hogging most of the space.

She told herself bracingly that she could look at this as one dream that did come true. She had the entire house to herself. It was large, opulent, a desirable property worth a small fortune and it was all hers, thanks to the generosity of her grandmother—and probably some pity.

But that was all right. She wasn't proud at this point.

Just lonely.

She listened to the silence and thought how nice it would be to occupy this house with a family. Right now there'd be a husband sitting up beside her, probably reading from the light of the bedside lamp, and a child calling for a glass of water. Charlen.

Impatient with herself, she punched her pillow and buried her face in it. There was no husband, no children, and she just had to live with it. And for the next couple of years at least, she couldn't afford the complication of either. She had debts to pay and a future to pull together.

So Blackberry House was going to be a bed-and-breakfast.

That thought brought Charlie Scott to mind. She rolled onto her back and closed her eyes, picturing him standing in the middle of her kitchen and telling her he still found her interesting.

She hated that it gave her a little thrill. But it did—a little curl of sensation in the pit of her stomach. A silly reaction, she thought, for a woman who'd been completely scammed by a man and was going to spend much of the rest of her life paying for it.

But she'd determined not to think about that. She would have her hands full getting the house ready for guest occupancy. There was no time for self-pity, but this was also no time to take risks. Loneliness was safe.

She closed her eyes, determined to be happy in her solitude.

KAREN AWOKE to the insistent peal of the doorbell. She raised her head off the pillow and squinted at the old clock on the bedside table. Seven twenty. Not a tradesman or the mailman. And many of her friends had left Bramble Bay.

She groaned, realizing that left only family. She leapt to her feet, grabbed her blue-and-white robe off the foot of the bed and pulled it on as she ran down the stairs.

The bell continued to ring the entire time.

This had to be her mother. A physician, now retired, Adelle Tillman's policy was to cause as much fuss as possible wherever she went.

Karen opened the door and was instantly enveloped in a White Diamonds embrace. Her mother loved Elizabeth Taylor and had adopted her signature fragrance as her own.

"Hi, sweetie!" her mother said, stepping back to look Karen over. "Welcome home. We thought we'd treat you to breakfast your first day back." The look in her eyes was very familiar to Karen; she'd seen it her whole life—love mingled with censure.

But Karen had determined when she'd decided to return to Bramble Bay that she wasn't going to let her mother get to her. She loved her, but her mom was always pushing. And Karen, at this point in time, had been pushed about as far as she was willing to go.

Her mother walked past her into the house.

Standing side-by-side on the porch were Karen's sister Paula, and Becky, Peter's wife. Becky held a pink grocery box on the flat of one hand and leaned way over a very advanced pregnancy to hug Karen.

"Hello there!" she said. She was dressed in blue denim overalls and a pale blue sweater that highlighted her silver-blond, porcelain-doll beauty. Her hair was shoulder-length and layered to frame her face and fall in graduating lengths from just under her chin.

Becky was the daughter of Bramble Bay's most influential family, and Peter was now business manager of Walker Electronics, the multimillion-dollar company Becky's father had started as a boy.

She was flawlessly polite and always behaved with grace and aplomb. In a loud, outspoken family, she was sometimes hard to take. She followed her mother-in-law inside.

Paula, in snug jeans and a short black leather jacket over a black turtleneck, folded her arms and looked Karen over. This was another look Karen was used to. A sort of how-can-I-fix-it-for-you look.

The twins were two years older than Karen, and Paula had always behaved as though it gave her the wisdom of many more years. Of course, she'd always been prettier and even smarter.

The twins had auburn hair and green eyes, a throwback to their maternal grandmother. Peter had freckles he hated, but Paula's complexion was creamy and flawless, her eyes wide and thickly lashed, her hair short and chic.

"So, how are you?" she asked, hoping, Karen was sure, to invite her confidence. "You've done all this so quickly. I know you're very brave and very competent, but you can't just launch into another life without taking some time to whine and carry on."

Karen hugged her and pulled her inside. "I'm fine. And whining and carrying on serves no purpose."

Paula was a psychiatrist. "I beg to differ with you, but it does. You have to get old stuff out of the way, or you build new stuff on top of it—and that gives you a poor foundation."

"Darling!" Adelle shouted from the kitchen. "Save that for clients who are *paying* you. Karen's going to build today on a devil's food buttermilk bar. Come on! I'm making coffee."

Paula rolled her eyes. Nothing brought the sisters together like a mutual exasperation with their mother.

Adelle had taken over the kitchen, bustling around in purple sweats, hand-painted across the chest and down the side of one leg with brightly executed pansies. Coffee brewed while she brought down plates.

Becky gathered silverware from a drawer and asked over her shoulder, "Would you put the kettle on for my tea, please?"

"I always do, dear," Adelle replied. "Though I swear that baby's going to come out fifty percent chamomile."

"But he'll be calm," Becky countered, distributing forks and spoons around the small round table in one corner.

Adelle filled the kettle, put it on the burner and turned it on. "He's half Peter, dear. The chances of his being calm are slim."

"He's also half me," Becky insisted, her tone polite though Karen thought she detected the subtlest edge to it. She looked to Paula for confirmation of that and found her picking through the pink box. Paula ate when she didn't want to deal with things. Karen had always thought it interesting that a psychiatrist could deceive herself like that.

"We know for sure it's a boy?" Karen asked, getting napkins from a cupboard and refilling the cat-shaped holder in the middle of the table.

Becky sat, eager to talk about the baby. "Yes. It's very clear. And he's perfectly healthy. There's no reason I shouldn't have a quick and painless delivery."

Adelle snorted as she carried a tray of cups to the table. "Becky, there's no such thing as a quick and painless delivery. Prepare yourself for that right now."

"Adelle, you had twins the first time, and—"

"A breech the second, I know, but I've not only had babies but delivered them and I'm telling you it doesn't matter if you have them standing on your head, in a sauna, or underwater, it hurts like hell."

"Mom!" Karen pleaded.

Becky looked pink-cheeked with distress. She responded calmly, though it seemed to require effort. "All I'm saying is that I've been walking two miles every day, doing my breathing exercises, and I'm calm about the delivery. So it might not be as bad for me as it is for many hyper, excitable women. And just because Damon is half Tillman, that doesn't mean he has to come into this world already needing Ritalin!"

Adelle seemed to have missed the message Becky was trying to convey and picked up on the one detail that concerned her.

"Damon?" she asked. "You're naming the baby after the devil?"

Paula surfaced from the donuts with a large, bulbous apple fritter and a groan. "Mom, that was Dam*ien*," she corrected, emphasizing the second and third syllables. "Damon has a nice sound. I like it."

Warming to Paula's approval, Becky added, "Damon Peter."

Paula sat down with her donut. "Even better. Mom, sit down. I'll pour the coffee when it's ready." She turned to Karen before her mother could take advantage of a break in the conversation. "You're definitely going to turn this into a B-&-B?"

Karen nodded, pulling a maple bar out of the box in the middle of the table. "I hired a carpenter yesterday. He's going to put a room divider right there for me…'' She pointed to the spot. ''Something very Victorian so that the atmosphere isn't affected, but conversation in the living room won't be spoiled by the sight of a messy kitchen.''

''If you're going to *have* a business in this house,'' Adelle said, ''you shouldn't have a messy kitchen. I worked for years and never had a messy kitchen.''

Paula lowered her apple fritter in exasperation as her mother poured coffee. ''You had a housekeeper, Mom. And you had all of us doing chores. Karen has neither a housekeeper nor children to do everything for her.''

The coffee poured, her mother sat down, clearly affronted. ''Is that how you see your childhood? One long period of indentured slavery?''

''No, Mother,'' Paula replied, leaning toward her on an elbow. ''But I did emerge from it with psychoses so complicated neither Freud nor Jung have classifications for them.''

''That,'' Adelle said with square-shouldered dignity, ''is because you look for motives in everything. I was busy and I needed help. That's all it was. If I overworked you, I apologize. If Danny changed his mind about your engagement, maybe the problem is his and not yours. So you shouldn't blame yourself and be such a fusspot about everything.''

Karen turned to Paula in complete surprise. ''Your engagement to Danny is off?''

Paula scraped her chair back, got to her feet, reached for her purse on the floor and turned to Karen with a shake of her head. ''Welcome home, Karrie,'' she said. ''Maybe you and I can have dinner sometime.'' She turned to Becky. ''Damon Peter is a great name. Don't change it.''

Then she turned to Adelle and pointed a finger at her. "I love you," she said. "But you would rattle God Himself. I have to go."

"Go," Adelle said, her elbows on the table, her hands holding a pottery mug. "Leave us alone to decide what to do about Thanksgiving."

Paula snatched up the rest of her apple fritter and a napkin. "We can't have it at my condo. It isn't big enough. But I'll bring Waldorf salad and a pumpkin pie."

"Pete and I could have it," Becky volunteered, picking at a blueberry muffin, "but if I go into labor in the middle of it, it'll kind of spoil things for everyone."

Karen patted her hand. "How could having our first grandchild and nephew spoil things? But we can't have you wrestling with a big turkey and on your feet all that time." She didn't believe the next words that came out of her own mouth. "We'll have it here. It's a big kitchen, you can all help. It'll be like when we were children and all came to Grandma's for Thanksgiving dinner."

She sat still as silence fell around her, compounded by everyone's stares.

"Okay," she said into the silence. "I don't cook very *well*. But a turkey isn't that difficult, and you'll all be helping me with the other stuff. And I've learned a few things over the last couple of years. I'm not as bad in the kitchen as I used to be."

Paula grinned. "It's just less noticeable since the requirement of smoke alarms in apartment houses."

Karen grinned back. "I thought you were leaving."

Paula waved. "I'll see myself out."

Adelle remained concerned. "Darling, are you sure? It's a big job, and you have a lot to do to get this place ready to open for business."

Now that the words had been spoken and couldn't be withdrawn, Karen decided she had little choice. "I don't have to worry about opening until January. I'll be fine. Maybe I'll practice a time or two before then."

"With a whole turkey?" Becky asked as though the idea was preposterous.

"Yes." Karen replied with confidence. "Then I'll give it to the men's mission, or something."

"Karen, those men already have enough trouble in their lives," Adelle said. "Even though your father and I are scheduled to serve at the community dinner for the homeless that afternoon, maybe I should—"

"I'm doing it, Mom." Karen took a bite of her maple bar and chewed and swallowed. "I'll buy all the ingredients for your cranberry nut bread and your sweet potato bake and you can come early."

Somewhat appeased at the possibility of being able to still control the kitchen if not the site of dinner, Adelle relaxed in her chair. "All right." Then she smiled at Becky. "But just to be on the safe side, if you want Damon Peter to arrive calmly into this world, you'd better have him *before* Karen cooks her turkey."

CHARLIE HAND-SANDED the scrolled carvings on the square column, then retraced the line with his finger to test for smoothness.

Satisfied, he stopped to admire one of the two columns he'd rescued from the old Whale's Tail Tavern two years ago. He'd paid a pretty penny for them, but he'd been sure he'd find the perfect use for them one day. And now he had. Karen Tillman's kitchen. With scrollwork brackets on each end and a row of spindles between, they'd make the perfect frame for the counter she envisioned.

The image of her face had troubled his sleep last night. He hadn't thought that much about her coming home until he'd stood face-to-face with her in the kitchen he'd remodeled and felt the energy that had ensnared him all those years ago. It was hard for him to believe that savvy little Karen Tillman had fallen victim to any man's scam. He couldn't help but wonder about the details.

Love had probably blinded her to obvious signals. It had happened to him. When he'd fallen in love with Vanessa, he'd failed to realize that the pursuit of the story, the love of excitement he so admired in her and that had drawn them together would inevitably tear them apart.

It had never occurred to him that the day would come when they weren't everything to each other. That she would tell him through her tears that even though he had to go home, to find something else to think about besides border wars, clashes for power, ethnic cleansing and the inevitable civilian pain and anguish, she needed to stay.

"At home they'll put me on some incumbent's campaign bus," she'd said, "or anchoring some magazine show. Here I can talk to real people, eat their food, live their lives, outrun the bullets with them."

But in the end, she hadn't run fast enough, and the bullet had caught her in the chest.

That was Vanessa, he thought, a twinge of old pain surfacing. *Running to and not from.*

He remembered his shock when he'd gotten the phone call from a colleague in China. "It's Van," he'd said, his voice quiet with respect for Charlie's grief. "She was with a group of student demonstrators when the army fired on them. She's not going to make it. And, Charlie—she's delivering a baby right now."

At first he'd been shocked. Shocked that Vanessa was dying and shocked that she'd had a baby. But there was no time to dwell on either. Military connections had gotten him a flight out of McChord Air Force Base, then one out of D.C. and he'd arrived before Ben was a day old.

Vanessa had died three hours earlier.

Everything had changed that day. He even felt as though his brain and his body had been altered. There was always a weight in his arms now, a small bundle of warmth leaning into him, depending on him.

And the search for the story that had always consumed his life now took a back seat with surprising ease to another interest that would allow him to be home most of the time.

He'd come home to Bramble Bay where his parents had helped with Ben's care the first few years. Then when his father's arthritis grew worse and the damp coast climate was no longer tolerable, his parents moved to Arizona.

Bay Carpentry was already taking off, so Charlie stayed on the bay and friends closed around him to stand in for family.

His life had changed considerably from his initial dreams but looking around at his shop and home in a restored factory at the edge of the woods, and knowing that in about an hour the school bus would drop Ben off and he would burst through the door full of news about his friends and questions for Charlie to answer—endless questions—it was easy to give fate a little credit for maybe knowing more about him than he did, himself.

And for putting Karen into the equation. She was an element he hadn't considered—especially back in the days when he'd been so sure his life would be about the adventure of learning the truth.

He'd since discovered that the truth about what turned world events, was not necessarily the same truth that fueled a life and gladdened a heart in the day-to-dayness of a man's existence.

There love was truth. And that wasn't something often found in global politics.

He couldn't help feeling a little smug that he knew that.

"Charlie?" Pete Tillman stuck his head in the door just to the right of the work table. They'd been friends since high school, and he'd been one of the first in Bramble Bay to come to Charlie's aid when he'd arrived home with a brand-new baby.

Pete held up two tickets. "Time to come through for the Kiwanis Harvest Dance. Ten bucks a ticket. Includes refreshments. How many dozen can I sell you?"

Charlie wiped his hands on a rag and waved Pete in. "Hi. I'll buy two tickets as long as I don't have to hang crepe paper again."

Pete made a scornful sound. "It'll take six tickets to get you off decorations detail, and I explained about the ladder. If I'd seen you hanging from the chandelier, I wouldn't have moved it.''

Charlie dug into his back pocket for his wallet. ''You almost killed me,'' he accused with feigned anger.

Pete was unimpressed. ''Oh, come on. The piano broke your fall. All you got was a sprain. And didn't Becky bring you and Ben casseroles for a week after?''

Charlie handed over a twenty. ''That was Becky. You did nothing.''

''I mowed your lawn.''

''It was November. It wasn't growing.''

Pete pocketed the twenty and handed over the tickets. ''Do you want to argue, or do you want to come to lunch?''

Charlie glanced at the clock. ''Ben'll be home in less than an hour.''

Pete hooked his thumb in the direction of the pub across the street. ''We'll go to Fogarty's. You'll be able to see the bus arrive.''

''All right.'' Charlie replaced his wallet and grabbed his jacket. ''But I'm not buying any more tickets.''

''You taking Joanie Carver to the dance?'' Pete asked, opening the door.

Charlie followed and locked it behind him. Joanie Carver was a wealthy divorcée for whom he'd built a wardrobe closet across the back of her bedroom. He'd taken her out a few times, but she wanted sex more than she wanted a relationship.

If he wasn't a single father, he might have considered that a plus. But with a child around who never missed anything, it wasn't safe. And he liked a little more style to lovemaking than her perfunctory approach allowed.

"No," he said as they sprinted across the quiet street. "We're not seeing each other anymore."

"How come?"

Charlie explained.

Pete shook his head as they walked into the dark, quiet pub, military music playing quietly in the background. "My God. What are we becoming? You're turning down sex, and I'm about to buy a baby seat that fits in a minivan! How did we get this civilized?"

"It just sneaks up on you." Charlie picked up two trays off the edge of the buffet and handed one to Pete. "You fall in love with a woman and before you know it you're in Kiwanis and selling your muscle car. All right! Brat and kraut today."

They sat down with their trays at a corner table under a poster of a country maiden with a very ample bosom picking daisies in a field.

"Becky cries all the time," Pete said worriedly. "For no apparent reason and without warning."

"I think that's a pregnancy thing," Charlie explained. "Unless she's not telling you something."

"No, she's been very vocal. Today it seems to be my mother. Something about our naming the baby after the devil. I don't know. She called me in the middle of a production crisis at work and she wasn't making much sense." Pete took a long pull on a nonalcoholic beer and shook his head. "I was hoping that Karen coming home might put a little balance back into the family, you know. She was always different from the rest of us, but she seemed to be able to figure out what was wrong when the rest of us were too impassioned to see it. But I guess they all had a big fight this morning at Grandma's house. I mean, Karen's house.''

"They?"

"Mom, Becky and Paula. Apparently they all went to welcome Karen and things sort of disintegrated. Mom's pretty pushy—maybe even more so lately than usual—Paula's defensive, and Becky bursts into tears even without provocation. I think after the baby's born I'm going to have to open a branch of Walker Technology somewhere in the Himalayas.''

Charlie passed him the hot mustard. "I could be happy about that, but you'd probably still be mailing me Kiwanis tickets.''

Pete frowned. "Could we get serious here? My child is about to be born into a hostile environment.''

Charlie made a dismissing gesture with his fork. "I don't think your family is hostile. They just have different ways of setting boundaries. Instead of knocking each other down like guys do, women try to outwit each other with words. Maybe you should just tell your mother to back off, and tell Becky to speak her mind.''

Pete looked at him as though he'd just suggested he drop a bomb on New York. "I'd be dead by nightfall.''

"Have you tried talking to your dad? Maybe he can talk to your mother.''

Pete considered that, then shook his head. "Dad would hate that. He's usually so...he stays out of family stuff. He just goes along but never really sets policy, you know?''

"Maybe he'd like an opportunity to change that.''

"I'm not sure." And Pete apparently didn't want to talk about it further. "So, who're you taking to the dance? Both my sisters are available now, you know."

"Danny and Paula broke up?"

"Yeah. Not sure what happened; neither one of them's talking. But it happened the night of Joanie Carver's housewarming. I think she figures in it somewhere. But I'd leave Paula alone. Danny'd kill you if you touched her."

Danny Halloran was another of their high school friends. He was a cop and though he was usually a marshmallow inside, he could be a bear in the line of duty, professional or personal.

Charlie laughed. "Paula scares me."

Pete nodded. "I hear ya. So, what about Karen?"

"She doesn't like me," he evaded.

Pete spread mustard on the bratwurst and methodically cut it into bite-sized pieces. "What do you mean? She had a crush on you in high school."

"Pete, it's no longer high school. A lot of time has passed and she's been through a lot. She told me she's not interested in a relationship."

Pete looked up, smiling. "So the subject came up?"

"Sort of. She apologized for verbally beating me up about the prom invitation."

"Oh, yeah. I'd forgotten about that. It's interesting though, that *she* hadn't. Don't you think?"

"I don't know. I never try to read women."

"Then how do you deal with them?"

"I don't think you have to understand them to deal with them. You just try to be kind, do what seems right, and keep calm."

Pete raised an eyebrow and gave him a superior look. "I know you were married for five years, but that remark leads me to believe you've never been in love. Because it's very hard to be calm about a relationship when you're in love."

Charlie had given some thought to that in the last few years. He'd thought he'd been in love with Vanessa. It had felt like love. But if it had been love, wouldn't there have been a way to work it out? Or maybe it had been love on his part, and not on hers. He didn't know. And now it didn't matter anymore.

"Maybe," Charlie said. "The point is we operate on different systems. We can come together in wonderful moments, but we can never see into each other's heads."

Pete leaned toward him. "Love is about hearts, not heads."

"We were talking about women, not love."

"Oh." Pete went back to his meal. "I forgot. I guess in my life, woman *means* love."

Charlie smiled over that, happy for Pete. A little depressed for himself.

CHAPTER THREE

KAREN WAS STUDYING paint samples after breakfast at the kitchen table the following morning when she remembered Hannibal. Her family must have frightened him away yesterday morning, but he had showed up for dinner last night.

She got a can of cat food and a spoon, making a mental note to buy more since there were only two cans left, and opened the front door.

"Hannibal!" she called. "Here, kitty! Here... Ah!" Her call ended abruptly in a gasp when she found herself face-to-shirt-button with a man. She fell back with a hand to her heart.

"Good morning," Charlie Scott said, glancing down at her from a small stepstool as he screwed the old carriage-lamp porch light fixture back into place. "Want to flip on the light?"

Drawing a steadying breath, she reached her arm back into the living room and worked the switch. The light went on. He'd replaced the bulb.

"Thank you," she said, turning it off again as he stepped off the stool. "Were you Grandma's handyman as well as her carpenter?"

"I was her friend." He picked up a folder from the wicker chair on the porch and handed it to her. "And I was coming by with the plans anyway. If you have time to look at them now, I can give you details. If you don't, I'll just leave them with you and we'll talk later.''

He looked fresh and gorgeous this morning in jeans and a simple three-button gray sweater.

She, however, hadn't slept well and was already wondering if she'd been wrong to come home. Her sister and her sister-in-law had both called yesterday afternoon to apologize for the morning visit, and her mother dropped by last night with a cookbook.

''I know Grandma doesn't have any,'' she'd said, ''because she was a natural cook. Never needed one. I thought maybe you could use mine.''

It had been a kind gesture with a barb in it—the sort her mother was famous for.

Karen had gone to bed thinking she'd been home just a little over twenty-four hours and her promise to herself not to let her mother get to her was already slipping.

''I really...'' Karen began to tell him she had a million things to do this morning when she was interrupted by the cat, who walked demurely up the porch steps then wound in and out of Charlie's ankles.

''Hey, Han!'' Charlie reached down to pick him up in one hand and lay him over his other arm. The cat closed his large yellow eyes and purred as Charlie stroked him. ''Ben says he lived with the family around the corner, but they moved away and left him.''

Karen reached out to scratch the cat between his ears. ''That's rotten.''

Hannibal drew his head back, sniffed her fingers, then butted his head against them, clearly asking her to continue.

She did, then put the folder on the wicker chair, opened the can and spooned the food into the bowl. Hannibal leapt out of Charlie's arms when he realized breakfast was served. He purred audibly while he ate.

"You got his morning off to a good start," Charlie observed. "I'm sure he's happy knowing that his meals will go on uninterrupted though the tenants have changed."

"And I'll be glad for the company." Karen retrieved his folder and opened it. She was about to tell him she'd look the plans over later when she saw his sketch on top.

It was a skeletal sketch of the living room, the kitchen in the background also fading into faint lines. But the room divider was drawn in boldly, exactly as she had imagined it...no, *better* than she had imagined it. There were columns on either side of it and some fancy wooden spindles at the ceiling completing the framing of the counter. He might have taken a photograph of her thoughts. She glanced up at him in astonishment. "That's precisely it!" she said softly. "Squared columns, the panelled front, the spindles at the top. Only I hadn't thought of the corner brackets."

He came to look over her shoulder. "The ornamental spaces in the corners are called spandrels." He turned a sheet of paper for her. "I've included a couple of other ideas on the chance you..."

"No." She shook her head as he showed her the second sketch, then again at the third. "No. The first one's perfect. That's *just* how I saw it." She traced a finger along the length of the columns. "You can do all that carving?"

"I retrieved the columns from an old tavern at the marina. Remember the Whale's Tail?" She nodded and he went on. "I'd always admired them. The place was torn down about three years ago and I bought some of the architectural details, figuring I'd find a good use for them. The room divider sounded like just the thing."

"Are they tall enough?"

"The tavern had ten-foot ceilings. You're welcome to come to the shop and see them for yourself before you decide."

The words came out before she could stop them. "Could I come now?"

She heard them and wondered what had happened to her excuse to go back inside without having to speak to him any further, much less spend time with him.

She didn't know. She just knew that his plan looked perfect, and making the house perfect in order to open it for business was going to help her get her life moving in the right direction.

His remark two nights ago about a courtship had to have been foolishness and flattery anyway. And she'd no doubt imagined the smiling determination that had gone into it. He seemed all business this morning, though he had a way of looking like seduction, even in jeans and a sweater.

He swept a hand toward his truck, parked at the curb. "Your carriage awaits," he said, collecting his tools off the stool and picking it up.

She pointed into the house. "Let me get my purse, and I'll be right with you."

KAREN REMEMBERED that the building that was now Bay Carpentry and Charlie's home had once housed the Blackberry Woolen Mills. They'd gone out of business when Karen was a teenager.

It was a long, two-story brick structure—a smaller version of so many old waterfront buildings in New England. The brick had been cleaned and the scores of small-paned window frames painted green. Pansies and fall crocuses lined the front of the building, adding brightness and color.

The old metal front door had been replaced with a wooden one with a fan window at the top and large brass handles. Charlie unlocked the door and ushered her inside.

His workshop was a vast open space with large tables covered with tools and standing equipment she didn't even recognize all around the room. It smelled like a forest.

Lumber was carefully stored just as she'd seen it in lumberyards, thick pieces standing, flat pieces placed on boards set wide apart to prevent them from warping.

She spotted the columns immediately near his workbench. They looked as though they'd been freshly sanded. She put a hand to one and felt the smoothness of the wood, ran a finger along the decorative groove.

"That was probably carved by hand a hundred and twenty years ago," he said, placing his hand just above hers. "Beautiful work."

"Where will you get the...spandrels?"

"I make those," he said and beckoned her to follow him, heading off toward a table across the room and under a window.

Two beautifully filigreed corner designs lay on the

table, connected by a dozen spindles joined six and six to a central design that matched the corners. Karen judged it to be about eight feet across—the width she'd envisioned her new counter to be.

"I'll mount them to a top molding that'll go on the ceiling, then we'll put the columns on each side of your counter and you'll be in business."

She touched the delicately turned spindles in the corner pattern. "It's so...perfect."

"I try. You can't sell bad work."

That was a simple philosophy, she thought, looking around the room at various projects under construction. But obviously one that had brought him success.

"How long would it take to put it up?"

"I'll need a couple of days to build the counter. I'll stain the columns and the fretwork here. A week or so probably to put it all together, then I'll stain the counter and we'll be set. You want drawers or cupboards on the kitchen side of it?"

"Cupboards."

"Then a week should do it."

"Is there anything I should provide you?"

"No, thanks. I've got tarps to protect the furniture. I'm very careful, and I never spill or splatter unless I *don't* cover whatever's nearby."

"I'll be sending the settee and the sofa to be reupholstered," she said, "so they'll be out of the way. All we have to worry about is the carpet. And the floor in the kitchen. And I'm going to be painting walls, so everything will be moved or covered."

"Why don't—" he began, but was interrupted by the ringing of the telephone. "Excuse me," he said, and loped across the room to answer it.

She studied the beautiful lacy pattern of the fretwork while he talked, then looked up when he called
her name. He pushed a Hold button, then hung up
the phone.

"I need some paperwork that I left in the house
for this call," he said, holding a hand out to her,
inviting her to join him as he walked toward his living quarters.

She went a little hesitantly as he ushered her into
another vast room nicely decorated in bright red and
dark blue in a sort of Americana style.

A rough, milk-painted screen sectioned off the living room from a large kitchen and a big farm table
with mismatched chairs.

"Find a comfortable chair," he said. "Or look
around, if you want to. Can't guarantee Ben's bed is
made, though. Here's a cup of coffee to keep you
going..."

He handed her a steaming mug, then snatched a
folder off the farm table and went to the phone on
the edge of the counter. "Joanie? Yes. Sorry to keep
you waiting."

The rooms had an appealing ambiance that reminded her of a large log cabin or someone's comfortable lodge. Karen wandered around with her coffee, peeking into the rooms that stood directly off the
main room.

What had once probably been the mill's adminis-
trative offices were now bedrooms and a third room
was apparently being used for storage. She passed
what must be Charlie's room—it held a large maple
four-poster, a tall dresser and a beautifully carved
armoire she wondered if he'd made himself.

She peered into what was clearly a small boy's

room with its bright curtains patterned with whim-
sical dinosaurs in primary colors, long, low book-
shelves packed with large, thin volumes, stuffed animals and other little curios, and a lidless toybox
spilling its brightly colored contents onto the floor.
Charlie was right. The bed had not been made.

But it caused Karen to stop and stare anyway.

It was built into the wall much the way beds were
on old ships, as though the occupant had been placed
in a sort of dramatic shadowbox frame. The sides
and top were scrolled and the bottom was the top of
the door of a storage cabinet built between the bed
and floor. It could be opened to allow the occupant
to climb into the bed, then closed to enfold him in
its cozy embrace. More storage took up the rest of
the wall and the whole had been painted white with
light blue highlighting the scrollwork.

Karen was sure that Ben loved it. It reminded her
of a child's version of the special protection she felt
in her bed with the gossamer draperies drawn around
her.

She couldn't help herself. She went inside, opened
the bottom cupboard and sat on the edge of the bed.
The spread, she noticed, as she tidied the foot of it,
matched the bright curtains.

How wonderful for Ben, she thought, to have a
father who understood so well what a little boy
needed. Then she frowned, wondering if it made up
at all for the fact that he had no mother.

As much as Karen's mother drove her to distrac-
tion, she remembered that when she'd been Ben's
age, she'd gotten lots of hugs and kisses, even though
her mother had been a very busy woman. Karen had
never had a sense of her mother having been up all

night and too tired or too stressed to listen to or comfort her.

She smiled wryly. It was only since she'd become an adult that her mother had become impossible. It was as though she'd dealt well with her children when she could order them around, but now that they were all functioning adults, she was like a fish—or an admiral—out of water.

"Have I kept you waiting so long that you need a nap?" Charlie asked. He stood in front of her with a mug of coffee, his eyebrow raised in question...or confusion.

"But you're smiling."

She stood up and handed him her coffee mug. Then she made Ben's bed.

"I apologize for intruding," she said. "I just had to see this wonderful bed up close. I have something similar, you know." She fluffed the pillow, then drew the spread over it and closed the cabinet door. The cozy cubbyhole was tidy.

She turned around to reclaim her coffee.

"You do?" he asked, still puzzled.

She led the way out, feeling suddenly confined in the smaller space. She needed the large dimensions and high ceiling of the big room. She chattered about the crown bed, thinking even as she talked that she sounded a little frantic. She finished with "I know it's not really the same, but the feeling it gives me probably is. Nighttime can be scary when you're a child. It makes you feel protected to be enclosed like that."

They stood together in the middle of the living room.

"But you're not a child," he pointed out gently. "Yet, it still scares you?"

Her impulse was to deny that quickly. It sounded juvenile. But she tried instead to explain what she did feel.

"I think I just don't like being alone in it," she admitted.

To her surprise, he nodded agreement as he sipped at his coffee. "I don't suppose anyone does. Particularly if you've shared a bed with someone you love, it's probably not fear of the night, but fear that you'll never find that again."

Yes. That was what she meant. But the fact that he understood was more unsettling than comforting.

"I should get home," she said. "I have a million details to see to before you bring my room divider in."

"Right." He took her mug and put it with his own on a glass coffee table placed atop a pair of large pediments and snatched up his keys.

The ride home was interminable and far too short. She couldn't get far enough away from him in the front seat of the truck, yet she could feel his body heat and some curious prickly sort of something running between them that she concluded must be energy.

To occupy herself when he stopped at the traffic light downtown, she picked up the folder off the floor of the truck and studied his sketch. She read the small, neatly hand-printed details he'd included on the bottom regarding measurements and materials, then for the first time, noticed the price.

She gasped loudly.

He jumped just as the light turned green and the

truck lurched as he slammed to a stop. "What?" he demanded, his arm going out instinctively to prevent her from pitching forward, despite her seat belt.

"I can't pay that," she said mournfully.

The car behind him honked.

He proceeded through the intersection and took the turn up the hill to her street. "All right," he said, expelling a sigh of relief. "We'll work something out."

"I mean, I know it's worth every penny," she went on, agitated, horribly disappointed. "I'm sorry, I just hadn't noticed. It was just so perfect, so...so..."

"It's all right," he insisted. "I have a payment plan."

"I have a budget."

"I have a *long* payment plan," he amended. "And I'm also the credit department, so don't worry about it."

"But you have to eat, too. No, it wouldn't be fair. I'll wait until I can afford it."

"No, you have to do it now, while your furniture's gone and you're repainting. You can pay me when you can, how's that?"

"It's not fair."

"I said it was, and it's my money."

"No, it isn't because I don't have it to give to you!"

He smiled suddenly. It was warm and affectionate and she found herself wanting to smile in response, but she forced it back.

He pulled up in front of her house. "I remember that's what I used to love about you in high school." He turned off the motor and unbuckled his seat belt.

"That passion for the moral high ground. I remember when we had Spanish Club elections and Mrs. Perez didn't think Connie Powell should run for office because she was pregnant. You rallied everyone to her support, even the school board."

"We needed her," Karen said, opening the car door. She didn't want to talk about high school. "She spoke Spanish better than anyone because her stepmother was from Guadalajara. And that has nothing to do with my room divider."

"It's the same principle at work." He stepped out of the truck and came around to her side. "I thought it was heroic then, and I find it charming now. But you're depriving me of my opportunity to be as generous to you."

HE SAW THE DETERMINATION waver in her eyes.

"I appreciate that you're concerned about my profits," he pressed, "but then you have to let me be concerned about your being presentable to open for business. If you're not a tidy cook, you won't want your guests seeing that when they come in to register, or sit down in the living room for quiet conversation."

She looked mildly offended and tried to step out of the car to challenge him about that. But she'd neglected to unbuckle her belt.

She rolled her eyes, reaching down to do it, but the buckle stuck.

"How do you know I'm a messy cook?" she asked irritably, still harnessed in.

Charlie leaned over her to work the simple mechanism.

"It's a little switch instead of a—" Words stalled

in his throat as he backed out from inside the truck and paused a moment to duck his head. The action placed their faces very close together, their lips about an inch apart.

He could feel her breath, could see the same excitement in her eyes that he felt.

"Central...button...." he finished distractedly, fascinated by the way her eyes roved his face then focused on his mouth.

She parted her lips to breathe or to speak, he wasn't sure which, but it was the moment he'd been waiting for.

He closed the tiny space and opened his mouth over hers. He braced a hand on the edge of her seat near her knee, and held the door frame of the truck with the other.

He half expected a slap or a shove, or at least an indignant refusal. But he was pleasantly surprised when her lips moved with his, responding hesitantly at first then with increased enthusiasm.

He wanted to know more, to push a little farther, but he made himself settle for what he had, remembering that she was wary and a little skittish, and he might very well end up with the slap anyway.

He slipped a hand between her back and the back of the seat and felt her hands come up to his chest, then move slowly along her ribs to loop around his back.

Then, abruptly, she drew back and pushed at the middle of his chest with the flat of her hand.

He ducked his head back out of the truck and offered her a hand down.

Her eyes were bright and a little angry, but he wasn't entirely sure it was directed at him.

"Thank you." She gave him a very regal look. "I told you I wasn't interested in a relationship."

"But you lied." That was ungentlemanly, but he couldn't help himself. "You felt very interested."

She walked around him and started up the little flagstone lane between the flanking rows of yellow mums. "I am not a messy cook."

He went after her. "Yes, you are. Remember the Spanish Club's Nacho Night to raise money for our trip to Portland to see Flamenco dancing? You lost control of the blender and there was guacamole on the ceiling of the cafeteria."

She stopped just short of the porch steps to give him a look of affronted dignity. "I had looked away for a minute, and Bonnie had removed the lid to check the contents without telling me."

"And there's nothing wrong with that, you know," he said, catching up to hold her elbow as they climbed the steps. "I'm nothing like the guy that stole your heart and your money."

She turned on him at the top, pain behind the confusion in her eyes. "He didn't *steal* my heart," she said angrily, then lowered her voice as two women, each pushing a stroller, looked their way as they passed on their morning walk. "He didn't steal it! Everyone thinks it's so clever to say he cheated you out of your money and your love. But it's not clever. It's awful. And the awful part about it is that I *gave* him my heart!" She pointed to herself. "I gave it to him! I trusted him and thought he was the best thing that had ever happened to me because he never criticized or even suggested there were ways in which I could do better. I believed he thought I was perfect. I fell for it all!"

He wasn't sure what she was telling him. The message was forceful, but unclear. "So...you're afraid to trust another man?" he guessed.

She seemed to think about that and finally shrugged as she walked toward the door. "That would be most women's reaction," she said, turning to look up at him as he kept pace with her. "But I'm not most women. I'm Karen Tillman, whose father is considered a genius among his peers, whose mother was president of the Oregon Women Physicians Association, whose older brother got so many A's in high school and college that his transcript looks like one long scream, whose sister was Miss Everything all through school and who still had time to get a degree in psychiatry!"

He nodded sympathetically. "A tough act to follow. But you're no shrinking violet yourself."

She rummaged in her purse for her key. "Yeah, right." She produced the key and put it in the lock while giving him a dry look. "I started a business with very little capital and grew it until I was a respected member of quite a large community with some rather impressive clients."

"Well, then—" he began, prepared to point out that she could certainly compete with her family, but she cut him short.

"And then I fell for a known con artist and lost everything to him," she finished for him. "It isn't men I don't trust anymore, it's my ability to distinguish a good one from a bad one." She pushed the door open. "Thank you for your offer to extend me credit, but I think I'll just live with the kitchen area the way it is. Goodbye, Charlie."

She closed the door in his face.

Good thing he'd once lost everything too, including his trust, and learned quickly that life couldn't go on without belief in something or someone.

He knocked on the door. When there was no response, he knocked again.

Karen answered, a scolding look on her face.

"Kiwanis is holding a Harvest Dance at the First United Church," he said into her forbidding expression. "The weekend after Halloween. Will you come with me?"

Her eyes widened in disbelief and she passed a hand in front of his face, as though testing for alertness. "Charlie, did your hear anything I said? I'm not—"

"You said you don't trust yourself to tell the good men from the bad ones," he repeated dutifully, folding his arms. "But I presume you want to learn how to, because that would mean you haven't let a bad experience kill your spirit. Because if you *didn't* want to—if you no longer cared—then that would be cowardly. And you're not chicken, are you? Not the woman who took on the entire school, including the board, over Connie Powell?"

She pursed her lips at him. "Don't think you're going to shame me or 'guilt' me into agreeing, because you're not."

Stubborn woman. "Then you have given up?"

"No, I haven't! I…"

"Then what time shall I pick you up?"

She growled exasperatedly. "What makes you think I'd even *want* to go dancing with you? Even if we had been attracted to each other in high school, we're different people now."

He passed his hand in front of her face just as

she'd done to him. "Hello-o. Weren't you half of that kiss just a few minutes ago?"

She heaved an impatient sigh. "That's probably just leftover attraction."

"Uh-huh. Left over from fourteen years ago?"

Even she had the grace to look sheepish about that.

"So, we find out for sure by getting to know each other again," he said.

"Charlie…"

"And we do that by you rehiring me to do the room divider, and if that's not too unpleasant for either of us, then you'll come with me to the dance."

"Charlie…"

"I'll be here Monday morning, eight o'clock. Shall I bring donuts?"

"No."

"Muffins?"

She was vacillating.

"Blueberry? Poppyseed? Cranberry nut? Apple…?"

She sighed defeatedly. "Were you trained by my mother?"

He smiled. "She did vaccinate me years ago. Set my arm once."

"Cranberry nut," she said, and closed the door on him again.

He walked back to his truck, thinking that he had a knack for picking high-maintenance women.

CHAPTER FOUR

"THE DINOSAUR ONE! The dinosaur one!" Ben jumped up and down in front of a tall round rack of children's Halloween costumes made of fuzzy fake fur. There were elephants, dogs, cats, pigs, rabbits and dinosaurs.

Charlie had come to PriceMart with the intention of finding something quick for dinner. He'd had a hell of a day at Joanie Carver's. He'd turned down her invitation to join her on a weekend in Seattle, so she'd made his life difficult all afternoon by insisting she didn't think the closet he'd made to enclose her refrigerator matched the wood in her kitchen cabinets.

Despite his assurance that he'd used the same stain as was used on her cabinets, she'd demanded he redo it. Then she'd made a fuss over the delay involved. He'd finally suggested she call a rival carpenter and left.

"Dad! Is this my size?" Ben had a death grip on a piece of bright green fur with a large darker green rick-rack trim to suggest the spine's bony plates. He was almost hanging from it.

Charlie ran to the boy's side before he ripped the body of the costume from the head. He reached up to remove the hanger from the rack and search for the size label.

"Medium," he read. "Six to eight."

"That's me!" Ben said eagerly. "I'm a medium. Let's try it on, Dad!"

He wore a size small, but Charlie pulled off the plastic covering, unzipped the suit, and helped Ben inside. A large stiff tail swayed a few inches off the floor, and a head with white button eyes and thick lashes, a big black nose, and a row of serrated teeth that were more amusing than frightening bobbed on top of Ben's head, then fell over it when Ben looked up at Charlie.

Charlie laughed and straightened the head, his bad day dissolving in the face of Ben's excitement.

"How do I look?" Ben demanded. "Am I scary?"

"You look great," Charlie told him. In truth the body hung a little on him and the tail would probably drag when he walked. "And I'd be scared if I was a caveman. But I think it's a little big. Let me see if I can find a small."

"I want to be a Stegosaurus," Ben said the big word with the ease of a child fascinated with the subject. "They only eat leaves. Is there a small one?"

"I'm looking."

There was no small dinosaur costume. In fact the one Ben wore was the only one on the rack.

"You're sure you don't want to be an elephant?" Charlie asked, knowing the answer before Ben gave it.

"No. It has to be this, Dad. I'll grow into it."

"By next Friday?"

"I'll eat double vegetables."

Deciding he was on to something, Charlie took Ben at his word and bought the costume. He could put wheels under the tail, or something. But he wasn't sure what to do about the loose-fitting body.

"Maybe Karen knows what to do about it being too big," Ben said from inside the cart as Charlie pushed it toward the truck in the parking lot. "Women sew, you know."

Charlie opened the tailgate and took a box that contained bread, cereal and coffee beans from Ben's lap and put it in the truck. "They do? All of them?"

"No. Some don't like to do housey stuff. Like cooking. They work, you know. They have cell phones and those computers that go on your lap and stuff like that. I think they pick on their husbands, too."

"Well. We don't want one of those." He tried to take the costume from Ben, but Ben held fast.

"Can I hold it on the way home?"

"Sure." Charlie lifted him out of the car, gave the cart a shove toward the cart rack and they both cheered when it went in. Then he unlocked the passenger door, flipped the front seat forward and lifted Ben into the narrow jump seat.

"I don't think Karen's like that," Ben said as Charlie snapped him in.

"How do you know?"

"Her business is gonna be a *house*," Ben pointed out logically. "So she's probably a housey kind of lady. And even if she can't cook, you can."

"What does that have to do with it?"

"I mean, if you married her."

Charlie frowned at him, wondering how he'd picked up on his attraction to her. Or maybe it was just speculation. Ben loved to speculate. "Why would I do that?'' He closed the door and walked around to climb in behind the wheel.

"To have somebody to kiss," Ben explained as Charlie started the motor. "Guys have to have a lady to kiss."

"Who told you that?"

"The Learning Channel."

And he'd thought Ben was watching the animal shows.

"Did you know that some guy stole all her money?" Ben asked.

The children's grapevine was amazing. "Yeah, I heard that."

"I'd go beat him up," Ben offered, "only he's in jail. And they don't let little kids in. I like the way she smiles at me."

Charlie found Ben's face in the rearview mirror. "How does she smile at you?"

"Like she really likes me. Some big people smile at you but you can tell when you get close that they don't really like you, they just want other big people to think they do. But her voice gets soft and her eyes are really pretty."

"Really." Charlie remembered with a wry smile the fits she'd put him through when he'd taken her home from his shop. "She doesn't do that to me."

"That's 'cause you're a man. Ladies aren't supposed to let grown-up guys know that they like them. I think it's a rule. So she probably really does."

"You think so?"

"You're going to do some work for her. So if you're real nice to her and she already likes you, maybe she'll get to love you." There was a very adult pause in Ben's speculations, then he added gravely, "And we could live with her in that house 'cause she says she isn't, but I bet she's really scared all by herself."

"You don't like the factory?"

"Yeah. But I think she'd like the house better. And we could still have the factory for your shop."

Charlie was alert to the importance of this conversation. His marriage hadn't come up once since Ben had been old enough to be aware that he *wasn't* married. Except when he'd asked about his mother, and Charlie had explained that she'd been a very brave reporter and she'd died.

"So, you'd like it if I got married again sometime?"

"Not to Joanie," Ben said without a moment's hesitation.

"Right," Charlie agreed. "To someone else."

"A housey lady," Ben said. "Who isn't too brave so she doesn't get shot. So she can stay with us forever."

"I'm with you there."

"I like Karen," Ben declared.

"I'm with you there again," Charlie said.

KAREN PUT ON A POT of coffee, watched the water begin to run through as clear as it came out of the tap, then turned off the pot, opened the basket and discovered a very wet but very empty filter. She added coffee, poured the water back through and began again. It was Monday.

She tied a bandana around her hair, berating herself for the state of her nerves. She didn't want a relationship with Charlie Scott and it didn't matter if he would be here in a minute to begin work—she wouldn't let him change her mind.

She started at the ring of the doorbell, took a moment to calm herself, then went to answer it. A tall, uniformed police officer stood there. He swept off his hat, revealing dark red hair. Light brown eyes in a freckled face smiled at her.

"Ma'am," he said, "I'm here to arrest you in the name of Ben and Jerry for overconsumption of Cherry Garcia. You've put production three years behind."

"Danny!" Karen threw her arms around her sister's ex-fiancé and drew him inside. He handed her an ice-cream bag. A peek inside told her it contained the flavor that had always been her downfall. She and Danny had both worked at Charlie's parents' supermarket when she was a senior and he was in junior college. She'd bagged groceries and he'd stocked frozen foods.

"Welcome home, Karrie," he said, giving her a bear hug. "It's good to see you." His expression sobered. "I'm sorry about what happened. How're you doing?"

"I'm fine," she said, indicating the furniture grouped in the middle of the room and covered with tarps, one wall half painted a cheerful butter-yellow, the others still the dull beige her grandmother had insisted went with anything. "As you can see, I'm well on my way to turning this place into a bed-and-breakfast. Charlie Scott's coming to put up a room divider for me. Very upscale."

He nodded. "I heard. Good decision. He's backed up a couple of months with work."

That wasn't quite the story he'd told her. "I have a few things that can wait..." he'd said.

"Paula told me about the breakup," she said, wanting his take on what had happened. "But she didn't tell me why."

He groaned quietly and shook his head. "Because she's an opinionated, conclusion-jumping, stubborn little so-and-so who thinks I'm fooling around with Joanie Carver."

"Who's Joanie Carver?" She had a vague memory of having heard the name somewhere.

"Divorcée who moved here a year ago. Husband was a plastic surgeon who left her for his nurse. She got a bundle, and she's trying hard to find a man to spend it on."

Karen studied him closely. "And it isn't you?"

He grinned and opened his arms to reveal his very unimaginative Bramble Bay Police Department uniform and his ever-present Mickey Mouse watch. "Do I look as though I'm somebody's boy-toy?"

"Then how did she get that idea?"

"We were all at Joanie's housewarming—she bought this gorgeous place on the other side of town. Anyway, Pete and Becky were there, Charlie, Paula and I and about a dozen others." He turned his hat in his hand. "I don't know what she was up to, but she was after me all night. I think it was because Charlie had upset her."

She felt an odd, uncomfortable, prickling sensation. "Upset her?"

"They dated for a while. He called it off, but she's determined to get him back."

She didn't like that at all, and knew it made absolutely no sense that she didn't. She remembered, though, where she'd heard the name. Charlie had taken a phone call from someone he'd addressed as Joanie when Karen had visited his shop.

She tried to concentrate on Danny's problem. "And Paula doesn't know they dated?"

He shrugged. "I don't know. I'm just tired of having to explain everything. Lately she's always ticked off about something, and I'm always having to pry it out of her and find a way to make it better. Isn't that some kind of syndrome? Shouldn't she put herself on a couch and have a good talk with herself? She's supposed to understand this stuff."

Karen punched his arm. "Danny! You're supposed to be in love with her. It's cruel to let her think you're messing around with another woman, even if she had been giving you a hard time. It sounds as though you two aren't communicating very well."

He sighed and put on his hat again, tugging the bill low over his eyes. "I'm tired of communicating. I'd like to just lock her in a hotel room for a couple of days and have my wicked way with her, but she'd probably find something wrong with *that*. No. I think she's thinking it's over."

"And you're not going to do anything?"

"At the moment, I don't know," he replied, and turned to walk out onto the porch.

Karen followed him. "Well, I want to hear a better answer than that the next time I ask you." She hugged him. "Thank you for the ice cream."

"My pleasure. Again—welcome home."

Charlie was coming up the steps as Danny walked down. They stopped at the bottom to shake hands and exchange a few football scores, then Danny walked toward his patrol car and Charlie came up, a bakery bag in hand.

"Ah," she said. "Muffins to go with the Cherry Garcia."

He raised an eyebrow. "Pardon me?"

THE WORK WENT WELL and relatively swiftly. From her perch halfway up the ladder, Karen glanced unobtrusively his way as he measured in every direction, then began to construct the counter that would be framed by the columns and the fretwork.

They stopped midmorning to have coffee and muffins, while he caught her up on local gossip and what he knew of their schoolmates.

They went back to work, then she warmed soup and made sandwiches for a late lunch.

She saw him glance at his watch. "Do you have another appointment? You led me to believe you had nothing urgent going, but Danny told me you're backed up for months."

"No other appointment." He took a bite of sandwich, chewed and swallowed. "But I have to get Ben from school at three o'clock. When I'm on a job, I usually pick him up and take him to the baby-sitter's. He doesn't like it because the other children she takes care of are toddlers, and he has to keep the TV down while they're napping." He grinned. "The *Rugrats* are better at high volume."

"Why don't you bring him here?" she suggested. This was not a good idea. It was setting a precedent of familiarity, the very thing she was trying to avoid, but she'd liked Ben. "He can watch TV in what used to be the maid's room off the kitchen and turn it up as loudly as he wants to."

Charlie looked surprised. "You wouldn't mind?"

"Of course not. I've got snacks and he can play in the backyard, too, if he wants to."

"Thank you," he said. "I appreciate that."

"Sure."

He'd finished his sandwich and was running his spoon back and forth to cool the soup when he smiled anew. "I should warn you, though," he said, "that Ben likes you a lot. He has a theory about women."

Karen looked up from her soup in amusement. "Already? I thought boys just considered little girls a different breed of boys until junior high."

"A lot you know," he teased. "Ben thinks you're a housey lady even if you don't cook much or sew."

"Housey?"

"Domestic. He must have gotten the word from 'housewife.' When he can't find or remember the correct word for something, he sometimes invents his own." He ate a spoonful of soup, then pointed the empty spoon at her. "The important thing is, he considers housey women the ones most desirable."

A little flare of excitement rippled up the center of her being. At first she'd been relieved when he hadn't brought up all morning the possibility of a relationship between them. By coffee break she'd found herself hoping, longing for some mention of it. But all he'd talked about was their old school-mates.

"Desirable for what?" she asked.

"Motherhood, I think," he replied. "I just thought you should know, considering your determination to remain single."

That wasn't entirely satisfying. Ben finding her desirable for motherhood wasn't the same as Charlie having feelings for her. Not that she wanted him to. It just made her feel alive for the first time in months to know that someone considered her something more than an accessible bank account.

She concentrated on her soup as Charlie was doing. "Well, that could work," she said, "if you'd let me adopt him."

"Sorry. We're a set. And you're against men at the moment."

She detected no indication that he was upset about that.

"I imagine that one day his fiancée will be surprised that his father is part of the package."

"Yeah, we've talked about that. I told him he can't marry anyone who won't let him set his father up in the carriage house."

"The carriage house? So you're planning to introduce him to debutantes with mansions? In Bramble Bay?"

His soup polished off, he put his napkin to his mouth, then dropped it in the empty bowl. "He's going to some Ivy League college that holds social events with Wellesley or Bryn Mawr."

"But those women are all probably headed for professional careers. I don't know how many 'housey' ones he'll find among them. At least until they'd had a chance to establish careers."

"Well, see, that's the thing," he said, pushing his chair back far enough to allow him to square one leg on the other. "When he grows up, he'll probably forget the 'housey' theory and go for looks and excitement."

She wasn't sure she had the right to ask, but she did anyway. "Is that what you did?"

He nodded, a sad smile coming and going on his face. "Somewhat. Vanessa and I met in college, and she was someone who wanted the very same things I wanted."

"Excitement."

"Yes. The thrill of learning the truth, particularly when everyone's trying to keep it from you. What I didn't understand in my youth was that in world affairs, the thrill of the search was beautiful, but the truth behind it was often very ugly. I saw people suffer unspeakably and die horribly and it changed something in me. I knew when that happened that I'd have to get used to the horrors continuing, and if that happened, my reporter's zeal would be lost. Or I could go home and report on Washington or some other home-front news."

"She didn't want to?" Karen guessed.

He nodded. "We'd been separated a lot anyway, so I'm not sure it would have been that different, my working at home and her being in the field. But she couldn't see it, didn't understand what had happened to me."

"I'm sorry." She meant that sincerely. She could understand what it felt like to think you and a loved one were on the same page then discover they were reading something else entirely.

He shook off the sadness and let his knee fall. "You live and learn. You start life appreciating a housey woman, then you forget about that when you develop and follow big dreams." He grinned in self-deprecation. "But when you have a few of them stomped on, you find yourself yearning for her again.

The best dreams become dreams of home.'' He spread his arms to indicate her kitchen. ''Like this one.''

Karen felt just a little shaken by his honesty. He must know himself well to be able to admit to that vulnerability. She realized with a little dismay that she was still protecting herself—and might be for some time.

So whether he teased her about their potential relationship or not, it didn't matter. It made her feel special and wanted, but not necessarily willing to do anything about it.

And this man was clearly working on his dreams of home. Someone to share his son and his home in the old factory.

For her, Bramble Bay was just a step toward safe ground on her way to somewhere else.

''Speaking of which,'' she said, briskly gathering up dishes, ''we'd better get back to work or it won't be anybody's dream home.''

He met her eyes for one moment, their expression indeterminate, then he helped her clear the table and went back to work with no evidence of anything lost between them.

But she felt something missing.

''That,'' she told herself sternly, ''is because you're an idiot!''

ALL RIGHT, so his psychology wasn't working. He knew she'd taken to Ben. His mention of Ben's theory had been intended to disarm her, to chip away at the barriers she'd raised between them and make her see the possibilities in at least giving their relationship a chance.

Then she'd asked about Vanessa and he'd possibly said too much. Despite the contemporary blurring of gender roles, many men continued to want "housey" women, and many women probably wanted men without vulnerabilities.

But he wasn't sure.

He went to pick up Ben and pushed the thought aside while his son carried on at length about the fireman who'd come to school to talk to them about safety.

"If your bedroom door's hot," Ben informed him, "you don't open it. 'Cause it means there's fire on the other side. And if there's smoke, you have to crawl on your belly."

It had been a long time, Charlie thought, since there'd been any heat in his bedroom. And he'd happily crawl on his belly to change that.

He patted Ben's knee. "I'm glad you were paying attention."

"I'm going to be a fireman!" Ben declared.

A brave and noble profession, Charlie thought. But in all probability, he could kiss his carriage house goodbye.

He was batting zero today.

The score improved considerably, though, when he returned to Blackberry House with Ben to find Karen standing on the kitchen table, her face white.

"What?" Charlie demanded, pointing Ben to wait while he went toward her.

She pointed at the floor while looking determinedly away, one hand fisted at her mouth.

Sitting in the middle of the stone tiles was Hannibal, looking very pleased with himself, a furry little

corpse in his mouth. A shoestring tail dangled life-
lessly.

Charlie did his best not to smile. "I believe that
in cat parlance," he said, "this is 'thank you for
feeding me.'"

"Could you tell him he's welcome," she asked in
a trembling voice, "and that mouse isn't on my
diet?"

Charlie reached for the cat, who sidestepped him
and ran along the edges of the room, searching for a
means of escape that would allow him to keep his
trophy.

"Open the front door, Ben!" Charlie shouted,
staying behind the cat until he picked up speed and
made a beeline for the door. Ben pushed it closed
behind him.

"That was cool!" Ben said with a wide smile.
"Hannibal can hunt!"

Charlie went back to Karen. "You can come down
now," he said, beckoning her with his fingers.

She turned to the chair she'd apparently used to
climb up. She must have kicked it over in her haste.

"You're sure he's gone?" she stalled.

"You saw him go out the door."

"What I didn't see was how he got in!"

"You might have a broken basement window in
the back. Or he might have sneaked in when I left
to get Ben."

"I hate mice!" she said in the way of a confession,
as though she were ashamed of it. "One of Pete's
friends used to tease me with his white mouse when
we were little. He'd dangle it in my face..." She
shuddered.

"Hey!" Charlie spoke sharply to get her attention.

"He's gone. Let's get you down from there before you end up in traction after all.'' He lowered his voice and coaxed. "Come on. We'll have a tea break and share the last muffin."

"I hope Hannibal doesn't get sick. God knows what diseases those things carry."

"He won't. Your grandmother got Hannibal his shots."

"How do you know?"

"Because I took him to the vet for her. Come on."

She came close enough for him to grasp her waist. Her hands went to his shoulders and he lifted her off the table, unable to do the selfless thing and simply put her down.

He'd seen this in movies and always thought it phony—a man supporting a woman's weight for interminable moments while her body literally slid along his until her feet touched the floor. The guy's arms would break, he'd thought. The woman would get hung up on the pen in his pocket or his belt buckle.

But the moment slowed to show him just how wrong he'd been. He could have held her forever, and he could have lived a lifetime on how it felt when her thighs slid down his chest, over his stomach, too close to that part of him that hadn't felt anything in too long.

Her flat stomach followed, closing whatever gaps there'd been between them, so that her breasts were close against him and at about the vicinity of his second rib, he felt their tips bead.

Her eyes held the same expression they'd had the day he'd unbuckled her seat belt, but this time he saw the memory form there of how that kiss had been, and the resulting eagerness to repeat the experience.

The moment could not have been more erotic had she been naked and lying in the middle of his bed.

Then she glanced over his shoulder and whispered urgently, "Your son!"

Charlie realized this was the first moment since the day Ben was born that the boy hadn't been in the forefront of his mind. Charlie refocused, though with a little difficulty.

He set Karen on her feet and turned to Ben. The boy's gap-toothed smile was brilliant.

"Now is she gonna make us a baby brother?" he asked eagerly.

Charlie heard Karen groan as she went to fill the tea kettle.

"Kissing doesn't make baby brothers," Charlie said, righting the chair that had fallen over.

"What does?" Ben asked.

Charlie thought he should have known better than to give him an opening. He took the coward's way out. "Getting married does," he replied.

Karen gave him an amusedly scolding look over her shoulder. "Ben, would you like some cocoa?" she asked.

"No! I want tea, too!" He shrugged off a colorful backpack, but a pointed look from his father made him amend that reply to "No, thank you. Tea, please."

Karen turned to Charlie. "Is that all right?"

"He's never had it, but why not? With sugar and milk, he might find it palatable."

They were a cozy little group, Karen thought, sitting around her kitchen table, sharing the muffin she'd carefully cut in three, and her grandmother's Blue Willow teapot filled with orange spice pekoe.

Ben told her about his day at school, then about his costume. He raised both hands, making them into claws. "I'm going to be a dinosaur. But not a scary one. A Stegosaurus. They eat leaves."

"Well, thank goodness," she said, then asked with a wink at Charlie, "So, when you come to trick-or-treat, I should give you leaves instead of candy?"

Ben looked horrified for a moment, then he said quickly, "They eat leaves *and* candy!"

"Oh, I see," she said. "Nice recovery," she added softly to Charlie.

"That's my boy," he boasted.

CHAPTER FIVE

A PERFUNCTORY RAP on the door Thursday was followed by Paula pushing open Karen's front door. She stopped just inside the living room, apparently startled by the chaotic state of it. Furniture was still grouped in the middle and draped with tarps. The walls had all been painted, but Karen had gotten only halfway around with a wallpaper border of full-blown pink-and-yellow roses with green leaves and vines.

"Wow." Paula's eyes followed the border as far as it went. "That looks beautiful. I didn't realize you were going ahead so quickly." She walked toward the room divider, mouth agape. "And look at that! It's really taking shape."

"I'm anxious to get this place open." Karen shrugged into her long, hooded green wool coat and snatched her pastel-paper-wrapped baby gift off the kitchen counter. "The sooner I get my life together, the sooner I know what I'm going to do with it."

Paula frowned, preceding her out onto the dark porch. "I thought you were opening this place with it."

Karen flipped off the light and locked and closed the door. "For now. But it's hardly a career, is it? I mean, I'm not contributing something really worthwhile."

"You're making people comfortable. Why do you always have to be…be…" Paula hesitated while she beeped open the passenger door of her BMW with the remote.

"Be what?" Karen asked as she got inside.

"Big." Paula climbed in behind the wheel and put her key in the ignition. "Why do you always try so hard?"

"Me?" Karen demanded. "What a question, Miss Double Major, Doctorate-in-Three-Years Tillman!"

Paula turned to her in the darkness of the car. They looked into each other's eyes and Karen thought that for the first time in their lifetimes, she felt something connect—some understanding take place that had been impossible until now.

"You're not competing with *me?*" Paula asked, her voice quiet in her suspected discovery.

Karen just couldn't go into that now. She was tired from painting, a little demoralized because she and Charlie were working side-by-side and it was all very friendly and courteous and upsettingly unsatisfying and she didn't know what to do about anything.

"Of course I'm not. Everyone knows the only true competition is with oneself." It was trite, but she hoped it would stop the discussion.

"You are."

"I'm not."

Paula turned on the ignition. The car sounded like old brandy would if it had a voice. "Well, don't," Paula said, checking her rearview mirror and pulling away from the curb. "I'm all show and no substance."

Karen studied her sister's profile in surprise. "That

must be why you have all those awards and citations."

"And no fiancé."

So that was it. "That's because you didn't let him explain."

When Paula gave her a surprised glance because she knew that, she said, "He stopped by Monday morning to welcome me home."

Paula sighed. "He didn't try to explain."

"You should have trusted him. But you made accusations."

Paula turned onto the highway and headed toward their parents' home. "That's an odd thing for you to say considering what's happened to you."

Karen had to agree. But she knew Danny hadn't come to see her just to welcome her home. It had been a silent plea for help with her sister.

"But you're more together than I am. And you're a shrink. You're supposed to understand people. Why do you think he didn't bother to explain?"

"Perhaps because I don't mean enough to him to warrant an explanation?" Paula ventured sarcastically.

"Right," Karen said wryly. "The man who pulled you out of a locked car that had fallen into the bay, revived you with mouth-to-mouth resuscitation and wrapped you in his uniform jacket and drove you to the hospital because it was faster than waiting for the ambulance, doesn't care about you."

Paula's expression grew grave, then she said with quiet grimness, "He just wanted the big cop award."

Karen punched her arm. "Paula!"

Paula glanced at her with a grim smile. "Don't

provoke me, okay? I'll need all my reserves to deal with Mom. What did you get the baby?''

"I crocheted him a baby blanket," Karen said seriously.

Paula glanced her way again, this time with a disbelieving look. "You didn't!"

Karen laughed. "No, I didn't. You know Grandma's attempt to teach us never worked. I bought him a silver spoon and cup, and the cutest little tuxedo you ever saw."

Paula shook her head at the road. "You scared me to death. I thought you'd gone and learned a skill that's always eluded me."

"The only true competition," Karen repeated, "is with oneself."

"Oh, shut up," Paula said.

After the games had been played and the presents opened, Adelle served cake and coffee. Karen and Paula rose to help.

"Do you think Becky seems a little tense?" Paula asked Karen as she sliced the cake onto plates Karen held.

Karen looked up to see Becky sitting on the brick hearth of the Tillmans' fireplace, surrounded by her gifts as friends helped her close boxes and make tidy piles of them. Her sister-in-law looked flawlessly beautiful in a high-necked pink dress, but Karen too had noticed a close-to-tears tension about her. She'd put it down to rocketing hormones and all the fuss.

"Oh, she just got all upset about the vote," Adelle said, putting a china pitcher and creamer on a tray. "Where are those sugar tongs?" She turned to rummage in a drawer.

"What vote?" Paula asked, still slicing.

"The one about the name." Adelle's voice was distracted as she rooted through the drawer. Then she produced the sugar tongs with a little sound of success and placed them on the tray.

"Not the baby's name," Karen said, still methodically holding empty plates to be filled.

Her mother sighed, clearly feeling victimized. "Well, what's so bad about that among friends? I mean, this baby is going to have to live his entire life with this weird name…"

"Naming a baby is not a democratic occasion!" Paula whispered angrily. "It's a decision made by its parents. Butt out, Mom!"

Adelle placed cups on the tray and began to fill them with coffee. "I don't see why. We're the ones who'll have to see it and hear it."

Karen and Paula exchanged a forbearing look.

"You don't get to offer your opinion on everything, Mom," Karen said reasonably. "Peter has his own family now."

Adelle's glance at her clearly disputed Karen's take on the situation as Adelle bustled off with the tray. She distributed coffee then came back for the tray of cake. Karen noticed she gave a particularly large piece to Becky.

Karen and Paula helped Peter pack the car with Becky's gifts when he and their father returned from dinner and a Bramble Bay High School football game. Becky carried plates into the kitchen.

"How'd it go?" Peter asked his sisters, pushing a toolbox aside in the trunk to make room for a boxed stroller.

"You mean before or after Mom took a vote on the baby's name?" Paula asked.

Karen handed her a smaller stack of boxes that she placed beside the stroller.

"You have to tell her to fight back," Karen advised Peter. "Or to stick up for her yourself."

When the three of them returned to the house for more boxes, Becky ran past them to the car in tears and shouting came from the kitchen.

"Yes, I think I *do* understand!" Ray Tillman said. He was a tall, big man with a handsome face, hazel eyes and a bald head with just a fringe of the red hair he'd bequeathed to the twins. He also had a big voice and was now using it at full volume. "I can't believe you're letting that get in the way. Leave the poor girl alone before your reasons become clear to everyone else, too!"

Adelle stormed up the stairs and Ray pushed his way through the door to the garage.

"I'm out of here," Peter said, kissing each sister on the cheek. "Tell Mom I said thanks for the shower."

"Coward," Paula accused.

"Damn right," he admitted. "'Bye."

Karen and Paula looked at one another in the darkened living room.

"What did *that* mean?" Paula whispered. "What 'reasons'?"

Karen sighed and shook her head. "Not a clue. Come on. Let's get this place cleaned up."

Karen filled the dishwasher while Paula walked around the living room and kitchen collecting napkins and discarded gift-wrap into a giant trash bag. They cleared counters, replaced the furniture rearranged to accommodate the crowd, then left quietly.

"What's happened to our mother?" Paula asked

as she drove through the darkness lit only by Bramble Bay's old globe streetlights. "Why is she even pushier than usual?"

"I don't know," Karen replied. "You're the shrink."

"You're the one who understands everyone," Paula countered.

"I'm the one who came home to figure *myself* out, remember?"

Paula made a scornful sound. "Well, work faster. This family's falling apart!"

Paula waited until Karen had unlocked the front door, then lightly tapped the horn and drove away.

Karen closed the front door behind her, enjoying the silent welcome of the familiar house, the smells of wood and fresh paint lending a sense of newness.

She gasped at a sudden movement from the tarp-covered pile of furniture. Hannibal, perched atop the stack, rose to his feet and stretched until he balanced on his toes, his back arched, his tail curling as he gave a mighty yawn.

"Hi, Hannibal." Karen laughed, inordinately happy to see him. His needs were simple, unlike those of the rest of her family. Or of Charlie Scott, who seemed determined to invade her already uncertain life.

"I suppose you think catching that mouse was your entrée into my life." She plucked the cat off the tarp and carried him into the kitchen where she filled a small bowl with water and put food on a plate. "Well, okay. You're the only one in my life right now that I understand."

Hannibal dug right into his food, purring loudly as he ate.

With his discovery of a broken window in the basement, he seemed to be trying to change his status from outdoor cat to member of the family with fireside privileges.

That was fine with Karen. Oregon was too cold and wet in the winter for anything to have to live outside. She'd found the broken window on a recent trip to the basement. She would replace the window, but talk to Charlie about installing a pet door when he was finished with the room divider.

It would be easier than letting Hannibal in and out—and it would keep Charlie around longer. An illogical consideration, she knew, for someone who wasn't interested in a relationship with him.

But a lot of life wasn't logical.

Just look at her family.

THE COLUMNS SAVED from the old Whale's Tail went up the following day on either side of the newly constructed counter between Karen's kitchen and living room. Charlie enjoyed Karen's fascinated attention as he fitted them in place, then secured them. The filigreed spandrels attached to an upper molding fit in between them with just the smallest tap of a cloth-covered hammer.

The room divider was perfect—if he did say so himself—a modern concession to tidiness in Victorian dress. Karen couldn't help a sigh of delight.

"Oh, Charlie," Karen said softly. "It's the most beautiful work I've ever seen."

Charlie stepped down the ladder, then moved it and took a few paces back to get the full effect. He could listen to her say that over and over.

Not the part about the work, but the "Oh, Charlie.'' He imagined her saying those words in that same tone but under entirely different circumstances.

"Looks pretty good.'' There was incomparable satisfaction in building something beautifully and well—particularly when the customer was as pleased with the result as he was.

"It's everything I imagined,'' she said, coming to stand beside him. He felt the softness of her flannel shirt against his bare arm, caught the whiff of a floral cologne, and the magnetic and complex essence of woman so absent in his life. He could remember vividly every soft convexity of her sliding along his body the day he'd lifted her off the kitchen table.

He fought a strong impulse to take her in his arms and kiss her senseless. She was skittish, but he was optimistic that she was drawing a little closer to him every day. He didn't want to do anything to change that.

He glanced at the clock. It was almost three.

"I've got to get Ben,'' he said. "Then I'll polish the whole thing for you and it'll be finished. I warn you, Ben will be higher than a kite. They had a Halloween party at school, so he's probably full of sugar and excitement.''

Then he caught a strong whiff of something torturously appetizing and asked, "What is that? Did I see you preparing a turkey?''

He'd been too busy most of the day for much conversation, and she'd been involved in the kitchen all morning and clearly preoccupied.

"It's a dry run for the main event,'' she replied. "I'm having the family here for Thanksgiving and I want to make sure I've got everything under control.''

She glanced away from him, color pinking her cheeks. She turned back to him with a forcedly casual smile. "I was hoping you and Ben could try it for me before you take Ben trick-or-treating tonight."

He wasn't sure what accounted for her embarrassment—her reputation as a cook, or the fact she'd extended an invitation to him with no coercion on his part.

He glanced worriedly toward the kitchen, teasing her. "Ah…"

She folded her arms. "I thought it wasn't in your nature to do the safe thing," she challenged.

"I was thinking of my helpless child," he answered with pretended gravity.

She rolled her eyes. "I wouldn't do anything to harm Ben," she promised.

"And me?" he had to ask.

She shrugged. "I might need you for other projects."

That sounded hopeful. "Tell me," he asked quietly, "that we're not talking about carpentry."

She shook her head at him. "Charlie…"

"Okay, okay. We'll be happy to test your rehearsal dinner. But you might have Danny standing by."

"Another crack like that," she warned, "and you'll need a cop."

He kissed her cheek. "Be back in half an hour."

He took pleasure in her instant blush.

KAREN FELT decidedly domestic as she set the table with her grandmother's Limoges and silver. She wondered if she'd been precipitate in deciding that a permanent relationship wasn't for her. She could do this—maybe. She and Charlie had gotten along well all week, she loved having Ben around, and she was beginning to notice how lonely the house was when they were gone.

Humming cheerfully, she went to the oven to check on the turkey.

Things took a negative turn several moments later when Karen looked up from her boiling potatoes to make sure she had butter, salt and pepper on the table—and discovered Hannibal happily ensconced in a tea-towel-lined basket she'd placed in the middle for rolls.

"Hannibal!" she shrieked at him, waving her pot holder toward the table. "Get out of there!"

He obeyed, moving like a rocket. The table seemed to explode as his hind legs kicked off, knocking one water glass into another, which in turn knocked the third onto a plate.

Glass and water flew, and china shattered in the wake of the cat's escape.

For a moment Karen could only stare at the rubble of her dinner table. What had been so beautiful an instant ago was now soaked and covered in broken glass and china.

She gasped as she contemplated solutions but finally could think of nothing but gathering up the ends of the tablecloth and carrying everything to the trash. She rescued the silver, the salt and pepper shakers, and the two unbroken plates, but the butter, the cranberry relish, and the olives and stuffed celery sticks were tipped into the can. She tried to save her tablecloth, but small pieces of glass cut her fingertips and thwarted her efforts so she finally forced it, too, into the garbage.

She concentrated on cleaning up the mess, the unexpectedness of it distracting her from the rest of her dinner. She didn't remember it until the hiss of potatoes boiling over caught her attention. With a cry of fresh dismay, she ran to the stove.

BEN BURST OUT of the school's double doors with scores of other small children, looking like an explosion of colorful animals. Every other family in town must have made their costume purchases at the same place because as well as several of the pig, rabbit and elephant costumes he'd seen on the rack, there was a veritable herd of dinosaurs streaming toward the lineup of waiting parents.

Ben, of course, showed the most personality. Charlie had inserted a wire in the tail to give it a little lift, but he noted with a frown that the body of the costume still hung on Ben. He'd tipped the head way back to see where he was going so that he looked like a dinosaur in the throes of hysterical laughter.

Charlie had to help him get out of the costume in order for him to be able to sit in the truck.

"But I want Karen to see me!" Ben protested.

Charlie tossed the costume into the jump seat. "We'll just put you right back in it when we get out of the truck. Was it uncomfortable?"

"It was a little hot," Ben replied as Charlie pulled slowly into the circular drive. "Do you suppose dinosaurs got hot?"

"Maybe. Of course, for them it was their skin and not a costume."

"Yeah. Like they didn't wear it over jeans or anything."

"Right."

"Are we gonna still have tea even if it's Halloween?"

"Karen's invited us to dinner. She made a turkey and all the good stuff that goes with it."

"Yum!" Ben exclaimed, then asked with sudden concern, "Can we still go for tea even when you're not working there?"

"I'm not sure, Ben. We'll have to see how things go. I'll be on other jobs and she'll have other things to do. She's going to open a business there, remember?"

There was a momentary pause, then Ben said hopefully, "She must like us if she's making us dinner."

That was what he thought, but he wasn't certain enough to presume anything.

CHARLIE KNEW something was wrong when he and Ben, in his dinosaur persona, walked up the porch steps to find the front door open and smoke swirling through the living room. An acrid smell greeted them at the doorway.

"She burned the turkey!" Ben announced as they ventured cautiously inside.

"Karen?" Charlie called. He flipped the switch that turned on the living room's Casa Blanca fan.

When there was no answer, he pointed Ben to wait by the door, told him firmly not to move, and went in search of Karen.

He found her working over a cutting board covered with white chunks of something...potatoes? She seemed to be slicing off a black side on each chunk.

She worked stiffly, her jaw set, the usually relaxed and beautiful line of her body tense and rigid. She glanced at him, her eyes moist, even brimming, but she tossed her head, apparently determined not to cry.

"What happened?" he asked gently.

She cast him another glance that told him to stay away.

He ignored her, but was smart enough not to touch her.

"Are you all right?" he asked, coming up beside her.

"I'm fine!" she snapped, then seemed to regret it immediately and looked in danger of losing her composure. But she did that head-toss again. "Though I seem to have proven to be the disaster-prone cook you remember."

"Karen..."

"I think I can save the potatoes," she said flatly. "And the beans are okay, though the bacon burned when I thought I'd turned it off but had it turned it up high instead. And the turkey's safe in the oven. But we'll have to eat in my bedroom so you don't die of smoke inhalation."

She gestured broadly to indicate the scope of the disaster, and he noticed that her thumb was bleeding.

He caught her hand and took the knife from her.

She tried to pull away from him. "It's just a cut from the tablecloth."

He held her fast and led her to the sink. "The tablecloth?" He soaped his hands to wash hers.

One tear fell, but she fought off more by telling

him an incoherent story about Hannibal, broken glass, burning bacon and Murphy's Law.

He didn't follow her story entirely, but it was clear that evil forces had been at work.

"I was feeling like Suzy Homemaker," she said in self-deprecation, another tear spilling over, "but I should have known better. I'll never be like my grandmother was, and I'll probably have to have breakfast catered when I open this place. Guests probably don't like to be awakened by smoke alarms."

He smiled, thinking she sounded as though she was regaining her good spirits. A lot he knew.

She looked at his smile and burst into tears. That might have upset him except that she wrapped her arms around him as she did it.

"I'm sorry!" she wept. "I promised you I'd never harm Ben, so I had to throw everything on the table away because there was glass everywhere! Then the potatoes boiled over, the bacon burned, the carrots stuck to the pan, and the rolls are incinerated!"

Ben appeared worried. "Dad?"

"Ben, why don't you go watch television," Charlie suggested, "while I talk to Karen."

"But, what's the matter with her?" Ben asked worriedly.

"She had a little trouble with dinner."

"But I want her to see my costume. That'll make her feel better!"

"She'll appreciate it more a little later."

"Will you tell me when?"

"First thing."

Ben skipped away.

Karen held on to Charlie more tightly. "I'm

sorry," she wept. "I never do this. But it's like every single person and thing in my life has or is a problem, you know?"

He saw that she'd built a fire to ward off the afternoon's chill, and he walked her toward it. The smoke had thinned, so he closed the front door, then sank down onto the Oriental rug in front of the fireplace and drew Karen down beside him, bending his knee behind her for support, keeping his arm around her shoulders. "Well, everything isn't your responsibility," he said reasonably. "You don't have to make everyone happy, or have everything come out right."

"Yeah," she replied, sniffing. He offered her his handkerchief. "But you'd have thought I could fix a turkey dinner. Friends are always telling me it's the easiest meal to prepare. Hah! Thank you." She dabbed at her eyes, then she drew a ragged breath as she studied the linen in her fist then said inconsequentially, "I didn't think men carried linen handkerchiefs anymore."

"Probably only men with messy little boys," he replied, rubbing gently between her shoulder blades. "Don't worry about the dinner. And it doesn't sound like it was your fault anyway. If I understand what you told me, Hannibal's the culprit."

"Sort of." She dabbed at her eyes and nose, then sighed again. "But how could I have forgotten all the other stuff on the stove? And turned the bacon up high instead of off?"

"You were upset and distracted," he said sympathetically. "And it was just a dry run anyway. When you do the real thing, don't put the roll basket in the middle of the table until there are enough people sitting around it to keep Hannibal away.''

She leaned into him companionably, both her arms wrapped around one of his. ''I wanted to do this right. In fact, if I was to be perfectly honest, I think I wanted to impress you.''

He laughed lightly, afraid to jar the fragile moment. ''I'm impressed. That was quite a disaster, but you saved the turkey and you didn't burn the house down.''

He felt her laughter against him, then her sigh. ''I guess I've always wanted to be what I'm not. And you just can't fight that. ''I'm not the super people my family are, and I'll never be the kind of woman who can provide a man with domestic bliss.''

Karen heard the timbre of his voice change. ''Sweetheart,'' he said softly, ''we men don't get our bliss from bacon in our green beans.''

She knew that was true, but she'd wanted so much to impress him. She sat up to thank him for listening to her, and for the sanity of his thoughts—when she saw it.

Banked desire.

It lay way back in his eyes, behind the kindness and compassion with which he'd tried to calm her concerns. She might not have noticed had their faces not been mere inches apart.

And something about the knowledge that her closeness made him want her, but that he'd still put that aside to help her—a quality certainly not in evidence in every man—made a desire for *him* she'd done her best to ignore since the first time she'd seen him again come roaring to life.

He must have read it in her eyes, because the emotion in his surged to the forefront of his gaze, darkening its blue to the shade of ocean turbulence.

She waited for him to touch her, but his arm behind her rested on his upraised knee, and his left hand was braced on the rug. This was clearly her move.

She made it, leaning into him and looping her arm around his neck. "Thank you," she whispered just before her mouth claimed his.

She opened her mouth over his, forgetting all the unsettled details of her life that always worried her and giving herself over to the moment.

She pushed him to his back on the carpet and kissed him with years of building fervor. Then she rained kisses over his ears, his throat, nipped at his chin and his jawline.

Sprawled across him, she felt every muscular plane of his body in contact with every curve of hers and relished the contact until even her elbow felt like an erogenous zone.

His mouth skimmed the soft flesh in the vee of her open shirt, then came back to her lips, soft and avid, and he kissed her so thoroughly that every shameful memory she retained from past failures was drawn out of her and destroyed.

She finally pushed herself up to her knees and pulled him with her, realizing for the first time that his head had been resting on bare wood.

"I'm sorry," she said, rubbing the soft hair at the back of it. "I didn't realize…"

"It's all right," he replied, leaning forward to kiss her throat. "I wouldn't have traded that moment for a down pillow."

"Dad!" Ben's voice came to them from the doorway of the back bedroom where he watched TV. He probably couldn't see them over the tarp-covered pile in the middle of the floor.

"Yeah?" Charlie called.

"Is Karen feeling better?"

Karen smiled a little wickedly. "Much better!" Karen shouted back to him. "Are you ready for dinner?"

"I want to show you my costume first," he said, scampering toward them across the vast expanse of floor. He appeared around the stack of furniture in his Stegosaurus persona.

"You," Karen said, getting to her feet, "are the most handsome dinosaur I've ever seen! Turn around. Let me see the tail."

She got to her feet, her deprived libido protesting vehemently.

"Something hurts right here," Ben complained, inserting a finger into the side of his headpiece.

She leaned over him to reach inside and remove what looked like a piece of corn chip. She held it up in front of his face.

Ben giggled. "Billy Fletcher spit his taco at me at lunchtime."

"Eeew!" Karen said, making Ben giggle harder. She took the handkerchief Charlie had given her and, finding a fresh spot, wiped Ben's ear then pulled the headpiece back in place. "How's that?" she asked.

Good." He nodded and the headpiece fell and bonked her on the head.

Charlie watched Karen and his son collapse into giggles, and felt his own laughter respond to theirs.

This was what he'd wanted all his life; the kind of family his had been.

He'd seen foreign families destroyed by border clashes and ethnic disputes, and he'd felt himself changing his mind about having a family. The children were so vulnerable, the parents who'd lost them, in such pain.

He'd come home to Oregon, but Vanessa wouldn't come with him, and that had contributed to his growing conviction that maybe families were no longer a good idea. Even some psychologists thought so. People needed the freedom to come and go as they chose.

And then he'd learned about Ben, and the moment he'd laid eyes on him, he knew what it meant to feel like a father—and with that knowledge came the indisputable truth that family was everything. Formed by blood or bond, it didn't matter. Holding together, loving each other, was all that would get everyone through.

He wouldn't let Ben lose Karen. And he would die before he lost her himself.

"You could come trick-or-treating with us," Ben invited as they helped her reset the table. It would soon be dusk, the darkness of the day bringing night on in a hurry.

"Thank you," she said, "but I have to stay for the children who come trick-or-treating *here*."

Ben accepted that reasoning, though he didn't seem to like it.

"And I got something special, just for you." Karen reached into a cupboard and produced a small plastic pumpkin-shaped teapot filled with candy.

"It's a teapot!" he exclaimed excitedly. "Dad, I've got my own teapot!" Then he seemed to recall their earlier discussion. "Does that mean we can't come here for tea anymore because Dad finished your job?''

She took Ben's face in her hands and looked down into his eyes. "Of course not. You are welcome here anytime. I'll always be happy to make tea for you.''

Ben looked relieved.

Charlie would have liked some detail on that promise.

Then, without warning, she straightened and looked into Charlie's eyes. She tucked her hands inside the bib of the overalls she wore.

"That harvest dance," she said, her expression daring him to gloat that she'd even brought it up.

He knew better, and answered her while going to the kitchen and looking for the potato masher. He found it in a pottery container of other utensils. "Yes?" he asked with no particular urgency.

"When is it?"

"A week from tomorrow.''

"Black tie?''

"In Bramble Bay? No. Just dressy.''

"What time?''

He subtly took control. "I'll pick you up at seven. We can have a late dinner afterward.''

She nodded and occupied herself putting the turkey on the table and turning the green beans into a bowl while he found butter and cream and mashed the potatoes.

Charlie couldn't decide if a simple dinner-dance date was a step forward or a step back from the hot kiss they'd just shared on the hearth rug. Then he decided it didn't matter. The date, like the kiss, was at her instigation.

This relationship wasn't as one-sided as she'd like him to believe.

CHAPTER SIX

KAREN DREAMED of driving a minivan. She took Ben and a half dozen other little boys to soccer practice. Two of them kissed her goodbye as they leapt onto the grass. They had dark hair and blue eyes and looked alike.

She took two little girls to ballet class. One looked like her and the other like Paula. They, too, kissed her goodbye.

She bought groceries, picked up the dry cleaning, came home and put a pot roast and vegetables in the oven. Then she went out again and picked everyone up.

The interior of the car was a cacophony of squabbles and laughter and silly childish jokes.

She called for quiet, but inside herself she was happy. More than happy.

Then she woke up to the quiet of a small-town Saturday morning. It was overcast and rainy, the kind of day that made the house as dark as early evening.

Hannibal lay on the pillow next to hers, curled into a tight little ball, head indistinguishable from tail in his total blackness.

She reached out to pet him, happy after her noisy dream to hear the cat's purr in her quiet house. His head came up and gold eyes opened to slits as his purr grew louder. He stretched one graceful paw out to her then lay his head on it and went back to sleep.

She remembered the utter disaster he'd made of her dinner yesterday, but somehow couldn't hold it against him this morning.

Not when she remembered that Charlie had taken her into his arms, comforted her, then kissed her as she'd dreamed he would all those years ago.

Ben and Charlie had eaten her dinner with apparent enjoyment, then left to go trick-or-treating.

In all the excitement of her disastrous meal she'd forgotten to ask Charlie about the pet door. But it was Saturday. Families played on Saturday. She would call him on Monday to see if he could work it into his schedule.

Meanwhile, she had floors and windows to clean, new linens to order for the bedrooms, small details to decide on to make the rooms cozy and inviting. That should take care of the several hundred dollars' credit left on her Morrisey's Department Store card. She'd held onto it since her college days, always finding something to buy when she came home to visit.

The weekend stretched ahead of her, long and lonely. Paula was off to Portland to a conference, Peter and Becky were going to a wedding in Salem, and she didn't want to see her mother, certain she would read the turkey dinner failure in her face.

Karen dressed in jeans and an old sweatshirt, made a pot of coffee and sat at the kitchen table with the Morrisey's sale catalog that had arrived in the mail several days ago. Hannibal had followed her down and curled up on the chair opposite hers.

But the doorbell rang before the coffee was done.

She went to the door, wondering if she was going to have to explain her ruined dinner to her mother after all.

But Charlie and Ben stood on the porch. Ben wore a yellow slicker, its hood shaped like a duck's head with an orange bill. Charlie wore a distressed-leather jacket over jeans and his big work boots. His hair was damp, but his smile was warm and brightened the day for her before he even said a word.

"We're going to breakfast," he said, inclining his head toward town. "Then we thought we'd check out the Saturday Craft Market, buy junk food. You know, all that good Saturday stuff. Want to come?"

She couldn't remember ever having a more appealing invitation.

"I should change," she said, plucking at the front of her sweatshirt.

"No," Charlie said, his smokey gaze making it clear he wasn't talking about clothes. "You shouldn't."

"I'm gonna have a waffle with strawberries and whipped cream!" Ben caught her hand and tried to pull her onto the porch. "Hurry up! I'm starving!"

She tore her gaze from Charlie's, went to the guest closet for her coat and purse and ran with Charlie and Ben to the truck.

The Bramble Bay Coffee Shop stood in the middle of a block of turn-of-the-century storefronts, brightly painted to attract local shoppers and the many travellers on the Interstate that went through town. The commercial area was four blocks long and looked much as it had when the town was founded in the 1860s by a cannery company. There was a new multiplex on one end of town, and a small mall on the other, but in between there were benches in front of the stores, barrels planted with pansies, and a boardwalk on the ocean side of the street.

She'd thought it old and backward when she'd been in high school, but enough time in the big city made her appreciate the cozy intimacy of Bramble Bay.

The coffee shop was filled with diners, the room abuzz with conversation and laughter. Charlie led Karen and Ben through a maze of tables to one of a dozen booths that surrounded the room. Ben sat with Karen.

The aroma of bacon frying, sweet things cooking, and coffee brewing was mouthwatering. Ben ordered his waffle, Karen splurged with French toast and bacon, and Charlie asked for sausage and eggs.

"Did you get lots of candy yesterday?" Karen asked Ben.

He produced a baggie of treats from his pocket. "Yeah! And I brought you these."

"Thank you." Karen explored the contents of the bag. "But there are peanut butter cups in here."

Ben nodded.

"Those are your favorites."

"I wanted you to have some, too. Dad told me to put the green apple candies in there 'cause those are his favorites." He smiled with a child's generosity. "It's our best stuff."

She wrapped an arm around Ben and kissed the top of his head. "Thank you very much. I'll really enjoy these while I'm working."

Across the table Charlie tried to look innocent, but Karen was sure he knew Ben's charm was working in his favor.

"Thank you, too," she said.

"My pleasure." His eyes were lazy and lingering as they wandered over her face.

She felt greedy for his attention, though she did her best to appear unaffected. She could feel heat in her cheeks, though, and was glad he couldn't see her fidgeting fingers in her lap.

"I'm glad you were free to come with us this morning," he said.

"Me, too." She laughed lightly. "If my dinner yesterday had been successful, we'd be too full this morning to do this. So I guess it worked out after all."

He folded his arms on the table and held her gaze. "We're ready to try again any time you are."

He was talking about the kiss, not the turkey.

"Yes," she said quietly. "Soon." And left it to him to decide what she was talking about.

After breakfast they walked along Commerce Street toward the empty railroad station used for charity rummage sales, and various other community projects. The craft market, held in the supermarket parking lot during the summer, moved indoors for the winter months.

Fifteen or twenty tables flanked the room, offering hand-dipped candles, homemade stuffed animals and dolls, hand-painted signs, jewelry, ceramics, hand-knit sweaters, baked goods and other treasures.

Charlie followed along behind as Ben and Karen went from table to table. Karen looked through everything with interest and excitement and Ben, usually impatient with waiting around, held her hand with silent appreciation for the moment. His son was becoming aware, Charlie realized, of what was missing in their bachelor lives.

"Oh, I have to have this," Karen said as she pointed to one of the many signs tacked up on boards behind the sign booth. It was about four inches deep but a yard wide and in blue letters on a pale yellow background read, Live well, laugh often, love much.

She turned to Charlie, her eyes lively with delight over her find. "Doesn't that sound like a B-&-B sentiment to you? I'll put it over the fireplace."

He came behind her for a closer look—and an excuse to put a hand on her shoulder. "It sounds like a life philosophy to me. Let me buy it for you as a business-warming gift."

She manacled his wrist with her fingers when he would have reached for his wallet. "There is no such thing as a 'business-warming,'" she said sternly, "and you're not going to buy me anything until I've paid you for your work."

"I'm not worried about getting paid," he said, removing her hand with his free one and approaching the table.

She held him back. "If you understood my financial position, you would be."

"I am aware of it," he said. "By Christmas everything that's mine and everything that's yours will be community property, so it doesn't really matter who buys this, does it?"

"Charlie..." she warned.

But her indignation gave him the opportunity to pay for the sign and have it wrapped.

By the time the vendor handed it to him, Ben and Karen had moved on to the knitted items and Ben exclaimed over a child-sized green sweater with a bold cat on the front that bore a strong resemblance to Hannibal.

Karen conferred with the clerk who checked a shelf of sweaters behind her and produced one in Ben's size. Ben was beside himself with excitement as Karen helped him off with his coat and pulled the sweater over his head.

It was a perfect fit.

"Dad, look!" Ben exclaimed, doing a turn for him. For the first time Charlie saw that the back of the sweater was adorned with the cat's backside.

Charlie reached for his wallet again, but Karen gave him a glare that might have withered a smaller man.

"I'm buying this for Ben," she said quietly, "or he's mine in the divorce settlement."

"There'll be no divorce," he returned.

She smiled. "Not if you let me have things my way."

He stepped back and let her pay.

They bought candy apples covered with nuts and chocolate chips and had them for lunch sitting in front of the fire at Charlie's place. After he'd finished his, Ben lay on his back on the sofa in his new sweater and fell asleep.

Karen covered him with a throw.

"He's in kid heaven," Charlie observed, smiling down on him from behind the sofa. "New duds, candy apple for lunch with his favorite person."

"You're his favorite person," she said, pulling off Ben's sneakers and tucking the blanket around his feet.

"He appreciates me as his father," Charlie admitted, "but he recognizes you as something important missing in his life."

She frowned at him across the sofa and his son. "You aren't going to start that again, are you?"

"You started it," he accused gently, "a long time ago. And you stirred it all up again when you came back."

"I just came back to find my place."

He spread his arms wide. "Here it is. Make yourself comfortable."

She shook her head at him, her expression exasperated but affectionate. He'd known he wouldn't be lucky enough that she'd take him at his word.

She turned away and walked into his shop.

KAREN WENT from project to project in the big room, trying to distract herself from a real, urgent need to walk into Charlie's arms and let tomorrow take care of itself. But he had a child, and while she and Charlie could survive a mistake, Ben might not.

She saw a chest under construction, an armoire, a shelf with pegs for hats or coats, what appeared to be a large flat box on legs.

"What is this?" she asked, leaning over it.

"Glass will go over the top," he explained, "and it'll be used as a coffee table. My customer has a lead soldier collection, and he wants this for a diorama of Gettysburg. Then he can display it without anyone messing with it."

"Excellent solution." She moved on, then noticed a cradle on a table near a window. It looked colonial in design with a squared 'hood' and rockers.

She put a hand to the smooth wood. It had been sanded but awaited stain. "Don't tell me Peter and Becky commissioned this," she said, pushing it gently to make it rock.

He came to stand beside her. "No. I just thought it would make a nice gift. The baby will grow out of it in no time, of course, but hopefully there'll be a long line of little Tillmans to use it."

"What a sweet thing to do."

He winced. "Sweet?"

She was amused by his reaction. "You take issue with being considered sweet?"

He shrugged. In his jeans and blue and gray flannel shirt he looked anything but. "That's kind of a simpering word, isn't it? I'd prefer thoughtful, I think."

"But thoughtfulness is sweet," she insisted. "And a pleasant surprise in a man with a lot on his mind."

They were less than an inch apart. She wasn't sure how it had happened, but she felt her body drawing even closer to his as though eager to bridge even that tiny gap. And her head tipped back, her lips parted...

"If it means you'll reward me for that," he said softly, putting a hand to her waist, "you can have it your way."

She reached up as his mouth came down on hers and their lips met with an explosive tenderness that reached inside her and seemed to scramble everything she knew.

"You can have this," she told herself. "Take it now."

Charlie raised his head after a moment, a question clear in his eyes.

"Take it now!" she told herself again. "So you thought you understood love once and you were wrong. Big deal. Mistakes are seldom fatal."

But there was Ben.

"No," she whispered regretfully. "Wait."

She expected impatience, even anger, but he

smiled instead and kissed her forehead. "Okay," he said wryly. "I guess I'm sweet after all. Come on. I'll put on a pot of coffee and challenge you to a game of rummy."

"I haven't played rummy in years."

"Good." He put an arm around her shoulders and led her back toward the residence. "We'll play for money."

CHAPTER SEVEN

"ALL RIGHT," Paula said from the other side of the slatted dressing room door. They were shopping for dresses to wear to the Harvest Dance. "Check this out. Are you ready?"

Karen, studying her own reflection in the three-way mirror and knowing this dress would also require new shoes, happily stepped out of the way. "I'm ready. Wow me with your gorgeousness."

Paula swept the door open and did just that. In ankle-skimming dark blue wool with a simple round neck, long sleeves and fitted waist, she was stunning. The soft fabric molded itself flatteringly to her shapely body and the color made a dramatic statement of her red hair and porcelain skin.

"You look beautiful," Karen said, hiding a tag on the shoulder by tucking it into the neckline. "Everything about it is perfect for you."

"It is pretty, isn't it?" Paula ran her fingers through her short hair, mussed from trying on clothes. "I thought maybe I'd have my hair done in the morning. You know, just a little flyaway style to make it look as though I tried, but not too hard because I have confidence in my own look." She made a face at herself in the mirror. "As if that were true."

"Why would it not be true, Paula," Karen asked. "Did you try to talk to Danny?"

"No, he hasn't called."

"Why don't you call him?"

"Because he told me I was opinionated and selfish and more interested in making a scene than learning the truth. And he didn't care if he ever saw me again."

Karen put an arm around her sister's shoulder as they studied each other's reflection. "Well, the first part of that is true. And the second was probably how he felt at the moment, but would probably reconsider now if you'd listen to an explanation."

Paula turned to her with a frown. "Now, how can you get away with saying things like that? I should want to hit you, but I just find myself wondering if you're right." She looked down at the red dress Karen wore as though seeing it for the first time. "That's a nice look for you." She took Karen by the arms and pushed her in front of the triple mirror so that her image was reflected on and on.

The dress had a deep V-neck, three-quarter length sleeves, and a cinched waist with a flirty flared skirt. The fabric was something silky with a tiny stiff piping at the very bottom that made the hemline ruffle.

"In the city, you always looked so professional," Paula went on. "And since you've been home, you dress like a farmhand. This should knock Charlie right on his T-square."

"Are you going with someone?" Karen asked.

"Jeremy Carver, Joanie's ex," she replied. "We're on the Traffic Safety Commission together."

Karen couldn't help her disbelief. "*You're* on a commission for traffic safety?" Her sister had a reputation for poor depth perception and a long history of mercifully small accidents. Except for the one she'd had at the marina that had landed her in the bay and been her reintroduction to Peter's friend Danny Halloran, now Commander Halloran.

"Yes, I am," Paula returned with a glance that told her she didn't appreciate the question. "My job there relates more to appropriate road signs, identifying problem intersections, helping to alleviate traffic bottlenecks."

"Uh-huh," Karen said, unimpressed with the distinction. Then she reminded herself that wasn't the issue anyway. "But that'll look to Danny as though…"

"I don't care how it looks to Danny." Paula turned her back to Karen. "Would you unzip me? I'm not doing it for how it looks, I'm doing it because Jeremy asked me."

Karen complied. "I thought he ran off with his nurse."

"That didn't work out. He's back. And all I want is a companion for the evening, not a life partner, so relax." Paula slipped the dress off her arms, walking into the dressing room. "My goodness, has Becky found anything to try on? She's been prowling through the racks for an hour."

Their sister-in-law walked into the dressing room area with a single dark green dress on a hanger and an air of despondency.

"Sorry to keep you waiting," she said as she disappeared into a room and closed the door. "I'll try to hurry."

"Don't worry about it," Karen called to her. "We don't have anything else to do today. All we're planning after this is lunch. And maybe a few minutes checking out shoes."

There was crashing and banging coming from Becky's stall.

"You okay?" Paula shouted.

"Define okay," Becky demanded with ill temper. "I'm a five by five woman in a four by four room. I can't even move in here without…" There was another crash and the contents of her purse came spilling out from under the bottom of the door, compact, lipstick and roll of antacids making it all the way to the wall, wallet and checkbook landing where they fell.

A descriptive curse filtered out from above the door.

Karen collected the items and placed them inside the cubicle under Becky's door. "Here you go. Take your time."

"I can't bend to pick them up!" Becky complained, sounding as though she were on the brink of tears.

"Then just kick them aside," Karen advised, "and I'll get them for you when you're finished."

As she changed back into her jeans and sweater, Karen heard silence for a few moments, the rustle of fabrics, more cursing. Karen was combing her hair in the three-way mirror and Paula was sitting in a corner, tying her tennies when Becky's door burst open as though it had been kicked. But Karen doubted she could get her foot up that high.

Becky marched out in the green dress and stood in front of the mirrors. The fabric was something shiny and stiff, intended more to accommodate a pregnant woman's size than to lend her style.

It had a strange little stand-up ruffled collar and

absolutely no other ornamentation. It fell to midcalf in a wide A-line.

"I look like a giant conifer tree!" Becky complained.

Actually, Karen thought, with her reflection reflecting itself endlessly, she looked like a farm of conifers.

"That's all right," Paula said, getting to her feet and coming up beside her. "A row of twinkle lights, a little tinsel, an angel in your hair and you'll be…"

Becky burst into tears. Karen wrapped her arms around her and glared over her head at Paula. "Becky, you can't expect to look like a size six when you're in your ninth month," she said practically. "Why don't you just wear that pretty pink thing you wore to your shower?"

"Because I wanted something new!" Becky wept petulantly. "Because I hate myself and everything and everybody! And your mother hates me! I don't know what happened. She used to like me."

"No, she doesn't," Karen assured her, patting her back as she continued to weep. "She's been treating us the same way. She's just…got her own problems."

Interested, Becky raised her blotchy, tearstained face. "What problems?"

Karen shook her head.

"I don't know. But you're not alone, so buck up."

Becky smiled thinly, patting her stomach. "It's hard to buck up." Her forehead puckered and tears began to form again. "Peter doesn't notice me, except to tell me to stop crying. He doesn't know what to do when I cry except tell me everything's going to be all right."

"It will be all right," Paula said bracingly. "In a couple of weeks you'll have a beautiful, healthy baby and life will get back to normal. Well. As normal as life with a baby is."

Becky sighed. "I'll never look normal again. Peter will never want to make love to me while I look like this. He hasn't touched me in more than a month."

Paula nodded sympathetically. "I haven't had sex in months either. Danny and I hadn't been getting along for a while, and I think the Joanie Carver party just blew it all up."

"Becky, Peter's probably just being careful, and you're being sensitive. But I've got you both beat." Karen reached into the stall she'd been using to get her jacket and purse. "The last time I made love, I woke up to discover that the man I thought I loved was gone and that he'd cleaned out most of my bank accounts." She pulled on the jacket and faced her companions one by one. "So let's quit whining and move on to something more dependable than men."

"What's that?" Becky asked.

Karen pushed her toward the dressing room. "Taco salads and margaritas. We'll get you a virgin margarita, Becky. Come on. Shake a leg."

"Yeah, right," Becky grumbled as she closed the cubicle door behind her. "I can't even *see* my leg!"

KAREN WAS NERVOUS. She was made up and dressed a full twenty minutes before Charlie was due to arrive to take her to the dance. She spent the extra time wondering what to wear over her new dress. The only outer wear she had was a somewhat dressy navy blue raincoat from her professional days in Seattle, and a green down parka she'd just bought for the Bramble Bay winter.

The raincoat was dressier, but protruded oddly over the yards of skirt. Not to mention that it wasn't raining.

The parka stopped at her hip, but made her look like a mismatched combination out of one of those books for children with figures on flip pages separated at neck and waist so that identities could be mixed and matched.

By the time Charlie arrived, she'd decided on the raincoat and thrown it over a chair. She went to the door, thinking that she'd never been this eager to see anyone before, Brian included.

Denying that she was attracted to Charlie and wanted to be with him was futile.

But that didn't mean admitting to it was wise. Their feelings for each other had the potential to change things. Every time he looked into her eyes, everything she'd ever wanted in this world seemed to fade and she was presented with new possibilities that had been unthinkable only months ago.

She yanked the door open and looked into his gorgeous, angular face, his blue eyes darkened by the white shirt under his double-breasted navy blue suit.

His gaze went over her new red dress, and given the way she'd kissed him only days ago, she was a little surprised when the look in his eyes was more adoring than self-satisfied.

"I can't believe," he said quietly, "that I get to take you to the prom after all." He handed her a florist box containing a corsage of baby orchids.

The elegant fragrance wafted up to her as she opened the box.

"I'd offer to help you pin it on," he said, "but I'd hate to do anything to hurt that dress."

"I can do it." She went to an oval mirror she'd just replaced that morning in anticipation of the arrival of her reupholstered furniture tomorrow.

His reflection just over her shoulder made her prick herself as she fastened the flowers. She winced and he took a step closer.

"Is Ben at the baby-sitter's?" she asked, for something to say as she gave it one more try.

"Yes," he replied, smiling at her reflection, "nose totally out of joint because we're going off without him."

"Poor Ben." She turned with an expression of sympathy. "We'll have to take him somewhere so he doesn't feel—"

She stopped. That sounded like a woman who intended to be part of his life for a while.

"That was just what I had in mind," he said, looking into her eyes, the confident male look she'd expected earlier now taking shape there.

He pointed to her coat on the chair. "This?" he asked.

"Yes." She went to him and turned around as he held it open for her. "I have to get something to wear for evenings. I didn't have that much nightlife in Seattle, and I didn't expect one here."

"Small town doesn't mean small living," he said, placing the coat on her shoulders. "The First United Church Hall isn't the Aragon Ballroom, but I challenge anyone to have more fun than the people of Bramble Bay."

He opened the door and she walked out ahead of him, stopping with a gasp on her front porch when she saw the horse and carriage at the curb, the driver in appropriate dress.

"See what I mean?" Charlie took her arm as they walked down the steps. "Isn't this cooler than a limo?"

"Well, I hadn't expected either." She moved ahead of him as they went down the walk. The driver reached back to unfold a set of steps. "I expected to go in your truck. Where did you *find* this?"

"I replaced the door for the community college's drama department. The Agriculture teacher provided the horse and is serving as the driver. He hires out for special occasions."

"Wow," Karen breathed.

Charlie helped her up into the carriage, then leapt up beside her, covering their knees with the plaid blanket on the other seat.

"Now I wish I had a formal opera cape, or something," she said. "With ruffles and ribbons appropriate to the carriage."

He put an arm around her. "You look perfect," he said, and when she turned to him, lips parted to object, he kissed her.

Life, she thought as she leaned into his shoulder, could not be more perfect.

THE CHURCH HALL was strung with grape-leaf garlands twisted with white twinkle lights. Wheat stalks wrapped with colorful ribbon flanked the stage, and tables set up around the room were decorated with colorful squash and gourds and tall candles with beaded lampshades.

The band, a collection of local people that included one of her mother's friends, and the man who'd reupholstered Karen's furniture, was already in the middle of a moody romantic number about moonlight on a bay.

Charlie took her coat to hang it up in the hallway.

"So, you're the missing Tillman," a woman's husky voice said from behind Karen while she waited for Charlie. "I've heard about you."

Karen turned and came face-to-face with a bleached blonde a good three or four inches taller than she was. At closer inspection Karen could see the dark roots of a spikey hairdo.

The hair stood up in moussed peaks and lay unevenly on her forehead. And managed, somehow, to flatter a beautiful oval face with green cat's eyes, a peaches-and-cream complexion, and a wide mouth painted a vibrant red.

She stood in spike heels, her black dress tight and short. Her black-stockinged legs went on and on.

Karen knew who she was before she offered a hand and introduced herself. "I'm Joanie Carver," the woman said with a bright smile, "and I just thought it fair to warn you that I'm getting Charlie back."

From across the room, Paula and Becky watched, openmouthed.

The need to appear unflappable in front of them allowed her to return the smile. "Really," she said. "From whom?"

A flicker of uncertainty crossed the feline eyes. "Come now," Joanie chided. "I saw you come in hand-in-hand. And I *know* him." She gave the word its biblical connotation as well as its generally accepted meaning. "He's feeling protective, possessive. A woman has to respond to that."

"I do. But I'm not after ownership in return."

Joanie looked her over a moment and shifted her weight on the spindly shoes, as though reevaluating an already-formed opinion. "So, you don't care for him?"

She was about to win this argument. It would have been so easy—and probably so expedient—to lie. But she couldn't.

"Yes, I do," Karen replied. "But he's not a trophy to me."

"You think he is to me?"

Karen took a little straight talk from her mother's book of social etiquette. "Isn't he? And Danny Halloran? You have a well-deserved reputation, Joanie, but, for the moment at least, *I* have the man."

Karen didn't realize Charlie had returned and stood beside her until Joanie's eyes swung to his, then back to Karen, battle preparations clear in their depths.

"For the moment," Joanie conceded with a smile for each of them. "But from what I read in the paper, you're not very good at holding one."

Karen patted Charlie's arm. "But I owe Charlie money," she said with a good-natured grin. "And I have nothing for him to run off *with*. So I don't think he'll be leaving anytime soon." Drunk with power, she turned to him and asked boldly, "Are you, darling?"

He was caught off guard, and for an instant she couldn't tell if he resented it or not. Then he replied quietly, significantly, "No, I won't. And it's not the money that's keeping me."

Joanie walked away.

Charlie's eyes continued to hold Karen's gaze and

she detected a glimpse of displeasure in them. "I don't know whether to yell at you for suggesting that we're here together because you owe me for a job, or to kiss you for calling me darling."

The scent of apple and spice candles wafted around her, happy laughter came to her ears from across the room, and twinkle lights lent the room a magical atmosphere. Added to that, she'd just stood toe-to-toe with what appeared to be a sensuously powerful woman and held her own. She was giddy with success.

She felt new. Different.

She leaned into Charlie and asked softly, "Do I get to vote on which reaction I'd prefer?"

She saw him fight against a grin and finally lose. "It better be the kiss," he said, then lowered his head and gave it to her as though they were the only two in the room.

It was possessive. Like a stamp of his ownership. But it was gentle and tender and felt as though it came from as deep within him as the depth it reached in her. That wasn't ownership. It was belonging.

"All right, all right." Paula pulled them apart, an envious look in her eyes. "There are teenagers here. We've got a table in the corner. Want to join us?"

A round table in the back of the room to the left of the band was occupied by Pete and Becky, George and Kitty Borton, friends of her parents who owned the stationery store, and a tall, handsome man with graying temples and Paul Newman eyes whom Paula introduced to Karen as Jeremy Carver.

Joanie's ex. Karen would have offered sympathy, but he had the boyish charm and magazine-cover smile of a man whose thoughts and emotions ap-

peared superficial. If he and Joanie had hurt each
other before he left her, he probably hadn't noticed.
And he seemed to like himself too much to be made
uncomfortable by the fact that a man who'd dated
his ex-wife occupied the same table.

Everyone danced. The music was mellow and a
little dated, unless you lived in Bramble Bay, whose
town and citizens were caught in a kind of time warp.
There were computers in every other home, but most
people had attended the same school and were taught
by some of the same teachers their parents remembered. They supported the same shops, voted in the
library as their grandparents had done, and came together for every occasion in the basement of the
church where they worshipped every Sunday.

As Karen moved to the music in Charlie's arms,
the lights went down so that only the twinkle lights
lit the shadows. She felt herself pulled right into the
spiral of Bramble Bay life, like Dorothy in the tor-
nado.

For several hours she lived in a different world
where there were no concerns about how she measured up in a family of overachievers. She wasn't
worried about proving anything to anyone, about filling her future with big accomplishments, about one
day moving on.

Everything she'd ever dreamed about as a snippy
fifteen-year-old with closet fantasies of Charlie Scott
was distilled in this moment when he held her in his
arms and talked about his life, his son, his plans.

She had no plans at the moment. Everything felt
so immediate, so *present*. She looked around at her
family and friends, felt Charlie's wonderfully competent but relaxed embrace and believed nothing bad

could ever reach her here. And if it did, she wouldn't be alone.

"You look so serious," Charlie noted, leaning back a little to look into her face. "Feet hurt? Where did you ever find shoes to match the color of that dress anyway?"

"No, I'm fine," she replied. "I bought them at Bedford's at the mall. They won't let us in there again, though. Paula ran into Danny and they ended up in a shouting match. Then Becky started crying when the shoes she liked wouldn't fit. All in all we made quite a scene."

He laughed. "It would be awful to be related to dull people, wouldn't it?"

"I wouldn't know."

"Did I tell you that my parents are coming for Thanksgiving? I told them I was taking you to the dance and they remembered you. Dad even remembered your campaign to let Connie Powell run for office. He let you put up a flyer in the market window."

"What happened to Connie?" she asked.

"She's a lawyer now. Did some work for me a couple of years back. Moved down the coast, I think."

Toward the end of the dance, the music grew increasingly romantic and slow. Charlie held her close, both arms wrapped around her. She looped hers around his neck and leaned her head on his shoulder.

She felt every one of his fingers through the thin fabric of her dress, felt the easy movement of his strong legs, now almost supporting her as well as himself because she felt languid and entranced. The fragrance of his cologne was all entangled with her perfume so that she almost couldn't tell which was which—or where her body started and his began.

And curiously she experienced no loss of individuality. It was a kind of symbiotic connection that gave her everything without taking anything away.

When the music stopped, she was still in Bramble Bay, but she didn't feel like Dorothy—or Karen—anymore.

She and Paula and Becky waited just inside the hall while the men went for their coats. They were heading off together for dinner at Porter's Galley.

"I can't believe the scene that Carver woman made all evening," Becky said as Paula took several steps away to greet a couple of friends. "She must have danced with and tried to seduce every man in the room!"

Karen had noticed. "Maybe she was trying to make her ex jealous."

Becky lowered her voice. "For all the attention Paula paid him, he might as well have come alone. Why did she ask him, anyway?"

"Probably to make Danny jealous," Karen replied quietly. "She denies it, but her behavior tonight made it pretty clear it wasn't because she's attracted to him."

"But Danny wasn't even here. He's on duty weekends."

"I know, but a couple of his buddies were here and they'll go back to work and talk about who was with whom. Word will get back to him."

"And...will that help?"

Karen shrugged. "Not as much as banging their heads together, then sitting them in a locked room and forcing them to talk."

The men were back with their coats, and Karen and Charlie made the trip to the restaurant in Peter's van. Karen found herself longing for the open-air carriage and snuggling close to Charlie under a blanket.

Porter's Galley was one of the few modern structures in Bramble Bay, a single-story building on the edge of a bluff, a wall of glass looking out onto the black velvet bay. Tonight there was nothing visible on it but the very distant lights of a freighter.

Before the party was halfway through dinner, Paula pleaded a headache and tried to insist that Jeremy stay with the party while she took herself home in a cab.

But he wouldn't hear of it.

Paula finally relented and they left together. Karen frowned worriedly.

"She'll be okay," Peter said. "She's just mad at herself for accepting that robot's invitation to make Danny jealous. And when she's mad at herself, she always gets a headache."

"You're Danny's friend." Karen poked at the radicchio in her salad with the tip of her fork. "Can't you make him see that if he explained about Joanie..."

"What good would that do now," Peter asked, "when she just spent the evening with Jeremy? I'm not talking to him about that. He'd only resent my intrusion."

"Peter Tillman!" Becky said at a volume that surprised everyone at the table and turned the faces of people across the room in their direction. "Do you really care that little about your family's happiness?"

She looked very stressed suddenly, the victim,

Karen guessed, of hormone fluctuation. Becky slapped her napkin on the table. "You won't talk to your mother, and now you won't do anything to help Paula. I suppose you won't be willing to talk to Damon, either! Fine time for me to discover this—a week away from delivery!" She stormed—or rather, waddled—toward the door.

Peter closed his eyes and groaned, then turned toward Karen and said in a berating tone, "Thank you, sis. Nice of you to light a match to her."

He ran after Becky.

Karen turned to Charlie, feeling guilty and depressed, and was surprised to find his eyes alight with amusement. "Well done," he praised, slipping an arm around her. "I was wondering how to get rid of them." He rubbed a thumb gently along her jaw in a soothing gesture. "Don't worry about them. She's his responsibility and he should have to put some effort into their relationship. Until this pregnancy, she's been so sweet and compliant, she's made his life pretty easy. This is good for him."

"My entire family is a mess," she grumbled, happy to lean into him. "I wish I had a magic wand."

He squeezed her shoulder. "I think you should stop worrying about them tonight, and just think about yourself."

"I am. They make the best praline cheesecake here, and I'm going to have two pieces."

"Good. Then after that," he said, turning his lips to her ear as a waiter poured coffee at the next table, "I'll take you to my place and make love to you."

Everything inside her seemed to spring to life. She became aware of her heartbeat, the expanding of her lungs, the working of her pulse. She looked into his eyes and saw all the love and warmth there she'd dreamed of in their high school days.

And then another glimpse of the humor that so defined him. "Provided there really *is* a cab still running at this hour. It occurs to me that your brother has stranded us."

"My house," she said, her voice barely a whisper, "is only a block away in that direction." She pointed to the west.

His eyes roved her face as though he was trying to read every small movement of her features. "Then, you're in agreement with the plan?"

She'd never felt more in tune with a plan in her entire life.

"Yes," she replied. "I'll even skip the cheese-cake."

CHAPTER EIGHT

THEY WALKED HOME briskly, arm in arm in the cold darkness. The air was crisp with the salty smell of the bay, the bite of approaching winter, and the aromatic woodsmoke that blunted winter's threat.

Water lapped against the bank and small things stirred in the bushes and trees along the road. A meow greeted them as they walked up the porch steps and Hannibal danced out of the shadows, clearly glad to see them.

"Oh, my gosh!" Karen exclaimed. "I forgot to feed him before I left." She unlocked the door and pushed it open.

"Let me do that." Charlie headed for the kitchen and pushed her gently toward the stairs.

"All right," she said softly. "I'm in the room at the far end of the hall."

He grinned at her over his shoulder. "I'll find you," he said.

He already had, she thought as she ran upstairs.

CHARLIE STRUGGLED to move calmly as he found a spoon, then a can of cat food, and fed Hannibal in a corner of the kitchen. He'd imagined making love to Karen since he'd held her in his arms on the porch the day she'd arrived in Bramble Bay.

He knew several issues lay unresolved between

them, but for now they were somewhere out there in the darkness. For tonight this wonderful home held only their renewed dreams of one another, and all the love brought back to life by their reunion.

He fed the cat, gave him a few strokes along his back, then closed and locked the front door. He flipped off the kitchen light and climbed the stairs.

He'd never been on the house's second level before and was not surprised, judging by the intricate woodworking downstairs, to find elegant door frames and crown molding upstairs as well.

Rosebud-sprigged wallpaper covered the walls, and a long narrow table stood against the wall between two rooms, a silk flower arrangement atop it in pink and blue. At the next interval on the other side of the hall was a small straight-backed chair.

The only light upstairs came from a room at the far end. Charlie stopped in the doorway at the sight of a large crown on the ceiling atop a walnut four-poster bed. Sheer draperies surrounded it. He remembered Karen telling him about it when she'd admired Ben's bed.

But Karen wasn't in it.

He walked into the pale blue room with pink-and-white accents, walnut wardrobe and desk, and listened for some sign of Karen. The bathroom door stood open, its light on, but there was no one inside. The soft light came from a blue Victorian lamp, fussy with fringe, on the bedside table.

Then a closet door creaked open and Karen stood there, naked except for a long, white muslin nightie held to her breasts and puddling at her feet. She smiled shyly.

"I was going to climb into bed," she said, her

voice a little raspy, "to let you know I was eager. Then I thought that might be too crass. So I was going to put this on." She made a small gesture with the nightie, but still held it tightly in front of her. "But that seemed a little artificial and sort of...staged. So...here I am." She shrugged a beautiful shoulder. "Looking for something to put on. I usually sleep in a flannel nightshirt. But you wouldn't want to see that. Would you?"

She pursed her lips, apparently aware she was babbling. He loved her lack of artifice.

He caught her bare arm and drew her out of the closet. "Maybe you're overthinking this just a little," he suggested.

Her eyes were huge in her pale face, gooseflesh standing out on her arms.

"I know. It's just that I've dreamed about this since I was fifteen."

"I've dreamed about it just as long. So there's no need to worry. I'm more eager than you are, but trying to be careful not to alarm you."

She smiled affectionately and he absorbed the warmhearted sweetness in it. "There is nothing remotely frightening about you. But you are overdressed if we're going to do this."

He opened his arms and held them away from his body in a gesture of defenselessness. "Then, do something about that," he suggested softly.

Clever on his part, he thought. Because if she intended to undress him, she had to drop the nightie she held.

"Don't think I don't understand the strategy," she teased, then fell in with his plan. She tossed the gown at the foot of the bed and stood before him like a vision in the soft glow of the lamp.

Her slender body was beautifully proportioned, firm, full breasts on a slim torso that tapered to a small waist. Her hips had a very feminine flare, but long thighs and trim calves and ankles gave him the impression of a flower on a stalk.

She pushed the jacket easily off his shoulders, and he watched the delicacy of her profile as her head bent intently over the French cuffs of his shirt. Glossy dark hair fell in front of her face and he tucked it back, the eagerness he'd admitted to held in careful check.

Both sleeves finally unbuttoned, she reached for his tie. Her tug on it tightened the loop around his neck and he asked in an exaggeratedly strangled voice, "Want me to do that?"

She giggled and left him to it. She pulled his shirt-tail out of his pants and, expecting her to proceed with the buttons of his shirt, he was surprised when he felt her fingertips inside the waistband of his slacks. Almost before he knew what had happened, he was unbuttoned, unzipped and kicking the pants aside.

Air was suddenly like a brick in his lungs and he had to concentrate very hard to maintain that control.

He pulled off his tie, tossed it at the pants, and with her competent help was soon divested of everything else.

Her eyes ran over him in what appeared to be shy fascination. Then she leaned into him and wrapped her arms around him, her little ragged sigh of surrender warming the spot just under his clavicle.

He enveloped her in his embrace, feeling as though he held the gift of...everything.

KAREN RELISHED the warm roughness of his chest against her softness and felt the tips of her breasts pearl against him. His hands explored her back and shaped the contour of her hip. Everything inside her rioted.

She tipped her head back to look into his face. "Would you mind if we turn off the light?" she asked. "Not because I'm embarrassed, but because I've always dreamed of us together in the dark."

His answer was to lift her into his arms and place her in the middle of the bed. He pulled the sheers back, then walked around the bed and turned off the light.

She held the sheers open for him on the other side. He climbed in beside her and caught her to him, warming her as the cool sheets wrapped around them.

The darkness intensified every sensation. She felt the gentle scratchiness of his beard, the callused tenderness of his hands roaming over her, the suedelike texture of male skin as she rubbed a foot along his calf.

It was everything she'd imagined as a girl, multiplied by all she'd learned as a woman. This was perfection without the uncertainties of inexperience. This was the man-woman connection with knowledge and maybe even a little wisdom.

His hands were everywhere and soon she couldn't think at all. Sensation took over her brain and her entire focus was on his hands working magic, then on his body rising over hers, claiming hers, transforming hers.

Love surged from him to her, from her to him until finally it simply bound them together, making something new of the people they'd been.

Karen held onto him, shocked by how different she felt.

NOTHING WOULD EVER BE the same. Even as Charlie rolled them so that she was astride him as they made love a second time, he knew some part of his stalwart, separate self had been lost the moment she touched him.

Some corner of his mind not overpowered with sensation understood the risk, but he took it anyway as he let her make love to him this time.

He was wild in a minute, but he let her take control as long as he could stand it, then when he saw her wicked smile as she reached to kiss him, he took the initiative and they came together with all the power of dreams suspended for fourteen years.

His hands clasping hers, he felt her tremors, heard her little gasps of pleasure, and felt that though everything he knew had changed, it was right.

Karen collapsed atop him, then curled against him as he pulled her into his shoulder.

"I love you, Karen," he said into her hair.

"Oh, Charlie," she breathed against his shoulder. "I love you, too. So much."

THE JARRING RING of the telephone awoke Karen in the middle of the night. She couldn't decide what it was for a moment until something caught her flailing hand in the darkness and put the telephone receiver in it.

"Hello?" she asked sleepily.

"Who was that?" her mother's voice demanded.

Still disoriented, Karen tried to brace up on her elbow but fell onto something hard. "Who was who?"

"The voice that answered the phone," her mother clarified impatiently. "Who was that?"

Karen had no idea what she was talking about until she realized what the hard something was under her. A shoulder. Charlie's shoulder.

Then she was boosted up into a sitting position and the bedside lamp went on. She saw Charlie on the other side of her bed, beautiful, bare back and right arm stretched out to the lamp. Then he turned back to her, hair sexily mussed, a frown between his eyes. "What is it?" he whispered.

She shrugged to indicate that she didn't know, then answered her mother's question. "Ah. That was Charlie Scott, Mom. What time is it?"

"It's 2:37 a.m.," Adelle replied, "and your sister is in jail, your father isn't home yet, and Becky says Peter isn't home either. What on earth happened last night, anyway?"

Karen tried to absorb all that unrelated but somehow commonly disturbing information and tried to pick one thing that could be brought into focus.

"Paula is in *jail?*"

"Jail."

"For what?"

"Indecent exposure."

"What?!"

"Karen, don't scream at me! I didn't arrest her.

And I can't bail her out because your father has the checkbook and is nowhere to be found—along with your brother. Can you help?''

"I'll be right there."

By the time Karen cradled the receiver and leapt out of bed, Charlie was already half-dressed.

"Who's in jail?" he asked as he sat on the edge of the bed to pull on shoes.

"Paula!" she shouted, running to the closet for her jeans and a sweatshirt. "Not only is this family going to hell, but now one of us has a criminal record!" As she yanked clothes off hangers, a frightening thought occurred to her. "Charlie!" she asked, turning to him. "What if I don't have enough money to get her out?"

"I've got it," he assured her, pulling on his second shoe. "We'll stop at the ATM on the way."

PAULA TRIED HARD to explain herself while Charlie and Karen sat with her in one of the county's two small cells.

She paced the small proportions of the room in a pair of orange coveralls with Winthrop County stenciled across the back. They'd been cuffed at her ankles and wrists and bagged shapelessly everywhere else. Her hair was disheveled, her face tear-streaked and dirty, her eyes red-rimmed and exhausted.

"I can't believe," she said to Karen wearily, "that I have to explain this one more time. I've told the story to two different officers, and twice to *Commander Halloran.*" She said the name with angry disdain. "And he didn't seem to understand it either time."

"You don't have to explain right now," Karen

said calmly. "We can just sit here quietly while they do the paperwork on your release and wait for—"

"Okay, I know it was all my fault!" Paula interrupted. "But I wanted to go to the dance and Jeremy asked me. I knew he was self-important and self-involved, but I had no expectations. But, my God!" She put the heel of her hand to her forehead as she turned and paced the other way. "Did you ever hear such prattle in your whole life? 'I could have gotten a BMW but I thought the Porsche really said *me*. I had to turn down Tyra Banks four times before she finally got the message. My tailor wants to use me as a model in a promo video, but I think I should get an agent to work the deal.'"

"So, you pleaded a headache and went home." Karen tried subtly to get her back on track.

"Right." Paula sat down beside her on the narrow cot. "But he didn't take me home. He took me to his place despite my pleas to the contrary. He tried subtly to get me into bed and when that failed, he tried not so subtly. I stayed long enough to get an ibuprofen and a glass of water, and called a cab like I wanted to do in the first place." She sighed, closed her eyes, and leaned against the white-washed concrete-block wall.

"And?" Karen prodded.

Paula opened her eyes and rolled her head along the wall to turn to her sister. "They don't run at night. I didn't know that. So I walked home. Two miles. He lives in the Brealand development on the edge of town."

"Why didn't you call me?"

Paula looked from Karen to Charlie, her expression sadly wistful. "I suspected what seems obvious by the fact that the two of you arrived together at this hour.'' Then she sighed and focused on nothing in particular. "Besides, I figured I had it coming. All the posturing, all the pretense…''

Charlie was glad when Karen asked, "Posturing and pretense?" He didn't get that either. "You mean with Jeremy?''

"No." Paula rested her elbows on her knees and her chin in her hands. ''I mean my whole career since I opened my own practice. People are so troubled, and there's really so little I can do. I want to have solutions and make promises that things will be better, but they're not getting better for me and I'm supposed to know what I'm doing.''

"Paula…''

"I was this pretty and smart girl, but when I grew up, I found myself terrified of making mistakes. I think because I never failed at anything as a child, I figured the law of averages would catch up with me and you deal with much bigger things as an adult. Mistakes then could have terrible results, and I always felt I was on the brink of disaster.

"I really wanted to be a physician like Mom, but if you mess up there, you could kill someone, so I went into the inexact science of psychiatry, because then if I did screw up, maybe no one would be able to tell. Except that people pin such hopes on me. I can't sleep anymore thinking about what they need.''

"You're a fine psychiatrist," Charlie said, going to sit on her other side. "I know several people who claim you've helped them. John Binder, for one, whose child died in that field trip accident. And Kevin Blye.''

She nodded. "Delayed stress from Vietnam and a hideous childhood. That doesn't just go away."

"You made him feel like someone cared and wanted to help."

She sighed. "I know his wife. That was more friendship than good psychiatry."

"What's more therapeutic than that?"

Paula smiled up at him finally, bleak humor in her hazel eyes. "Want to run away with me?"

Karen elbowed her. "You didn't finish your story. Did you take your clothes off while you were walking home, or what?"

Paula curled both legs up cross-legged on the cot. "I got home about one and went to bed. Just before two I heard someone pounding on my door. I threw a robe on and went to the door before the sound woke my neighbors." To Charlie, she explained, "I live in the Bayside Condos. Six of us share a common hallway." She rubbed her eyes and continued. "It was Jeremy Carver. Apparently when I proved recalcitrant earlier, he went to see Joanie, thinking he could talk her around to restoring his husbandly rights, at least for tonight, but she threw him out, so he thought he'd try me again."

"And you took your clothes off to discourage him?" Karen asked.

Paula gave her a dark look. "No, I did not. But by this time all my neighbors were in the hallway complaining about the disturbance. I walked Jeremy to the elevator and told him to go home and sleep it off. As I was walking back to my door, he grabbed the back of my robe and…you know…silk on silk. The belt opened and I walked right out of it—at the same moment that Danny arrived, responding to a call to the Bramble Bay PD by Mrs. Fennerman. He arrested me.'' She folded her arms and added on a grumble, "And I know he enjoyed it!"

"I was just doing my job," Danny said as he unlocked the cell door and opened it wide. "You're free to go…if you want to go."

Paula stood wearily, a confused expression on her face. "If I *want* to go?"

Danny folded his arms, the leather of his utility belt creaking. His features were stiff, but there was something conciliatory in the depths of his eyes. He glanced at his watch. "Hal Johnson's coming in in five minutes to cover the rest of my shift." He heaved a deep sigh, as though this was difficult for him. "If you want to invite me for coffee, or come to my place, I'll explain about Joanie Carver."

Charlie and Karen moved aside as Paula took several hesitant steps toward him. "I just spent the evening with Jeremy Carver at the dance," she said.

He nodded glumly. "Yeah, I heard."

Paula took another step. "I can almost understand her behavior. He's like being with an egotistical robot."

"I gave her no encouragement that night. She was just mad at Charlie and trying to soothe her ego with me."

"She was all over you," Paula insisted.

"I pushed her away," Danny returned. "Several times. And when you found us in her bedroom, it was because I'd gone to get our coats to get us the hell out of there."

"Our coats," Paula said, "were in the library."

Danny spread his arms in exasperation. "So, give me life without parole. I didn't know that! How

many houses do *you* know that have a library these
days? My mother always put guests' coats in the bedroom.''

"Karen's has a library," Paula said.

Danny dropped his arms and nodded, looking as
though he was certain he'd just lost this discussion.

"And she'd probably show it to you," Paula continued as she covered the last few steps that separated
them, "when you join us for Thanksgiving dinner."

It took him a moment to realize what that meant.
Then he smiled and touched a hand to her arm.
"About the coffee."

"My place." She turned her hand to catch his.
"I'll wait in your car."

Paula excused herself to use the ladies' room.

"When do I get my bail money back?" Karen
asked Danny practically.

He took an envelope out of his hip pocket and
handed it to her. "Right now."

Karen looked in it, then up at him in surprise.
"But, don't you have to keep it until she appears in
court or something?"

Danny glanced in the direction Paula had taken,
then replied quietly, "No court, no charges filed, no
bail necessary."

"Then...?"

"I had her behind bars," he said. "And I wasn't
letting her go until I could talk to her. Waiting for
bail money was a good way to keep her here."

"That's criminal," Karen chided, "but insidiously
clever. Good work, Danny."

He took a small bow. "Sorry to get you up in the
middle of the night, but I hoped you'd understand."

Charlie threatened him with a look. "You owe me

a pair of Trailblazer tickets, or something of equal value, or I'm squealing to the commissioner. I just finished rebuilding his deck, you know. We're on pretty good terms."

Danny's eyes went from Charlie to Karen then back again, clearly understanding what his plan had interrupted. He smiled. "Sorry," he said, with no visible evidence in his expression that that was true.

"Yeah. Good luck with coffee." Charlie put an arm around Karen's shoulders and led her from the jail. It was just after 4:00 a.m.

"WANT ME TO DRIVE?" Charlie asked Karen as they approached her car. "You look exhausted."

She handed him the keys and smiled weakly. "Nothing tarnishes the afterglow like bailing someone out of jail in the middle of the night."

He caught her arm as she would have walked around the car to the passenger side. "Nothing's tarnished," he said, giving her a swift kiss. "You look *beautiful* but exhausted. How's that?"

She took a moment to wrap her arms around him and just hold on. "Nice try. I can't wait to get back to bed."

"Yeah, me, too."

Charlie drove home in silence. They pulled off their clothes and climbed into bed, meeting in the soft cool middle and wrapping themselves sleepily in each other's arms.

Karen sighed against Charlie's shoulder. "I can't believe that really happened."

"It had a happy ending," Charlie said drowsily.

"Yeah. So it seems."

"We can have a double wedding."

Karen punched his chest and they fell asleep.

SHE AWOKE to the sound of the shower just before seven o'clock. She wrapped her arms around herself, missing Charlie's arms and smiling over the memory of how beautiful the night had been—the trip to jail notwithstanding.

Knowing Charlie would have to be off soon to pick up Ben from the baby-sitter's, she pulled on the jeans and sweatshirt she'd discarded early this morning and ran downstairs to make breakfast. Well—to put out cereal and fruit and make a pot of coffee.

The sound of her doorbell startled her into looking at the clock. 7:05. Who could that be this early in the morning?

Paula? she wondered, going to the door. Maybe the reconciliation hadn't worked after all and she...

It was not Paula.

It was a tall, handsome man with beautifully styled dark blond hair and gray eyes. He wore a camel-colored alpaca topcoat, a light blue turtleneck visible above the collar.

He smiled warmly and said, his voice a soft embrace, "Karen! God. My favorite memories are of you at this hour, hair all over the place, dressed in grubbies, trying to get yourself together for the day ahead."

Karen stared at him in complete disbelief, half convinced that he was an hallucination from her eventful night and little sleep.

She closed her eyes, then opened them again, but Brian Spencer was still there on her front porch. Big as life. Big as the heartache and humiliation he'd caused her. The world—her life—seemed to tip onto its side. Things spilled out—things she'd thought she was coming to understand.

"I put you in jail," she said, still holding the door to prevent his entry.

He shrugged and smiled his charming smile. "Some legal technicality about my representation. I didn't get it entirely. But I'm out."

"Out?" She struggled to stand the world back up again, grasping at one of the few details about his conviction that she'd chosen to remember. "You owe me…" She named a figure that still had the ability to rattle her nerve endings when she thought about it.

He nodded amenably. "That's why I'm here."

"To pay me back?" She felt an instant's hope, a sense of justice realized.

He decimated that hope with a shake of his head. "I'm afraid not. At the moment I have no job and no place to live, but I thought since it's in your best interest to see that I get on my feet again, you might give me a place to stay while I look for work. Maybe cab fare to— Oof!"

Karen pushed him so hard with both hands that he went head over hindmost all the way down to the walk.

She followed him, temper bursting up through her like steam in a pipe—valve wide-open. The morning was cold and threatening rain, but she didn't notice.

"You idiot!" she shouted at him. "How do you even *dare* come here with a suggestion like that?"

Brian got carefully to his feet, taking two steps back from her as he brushed himself off, an air of hurt feelings about him.

"I thought after all we'd been to each other—"

"To each other?" she demanded. "You lied to me! You stole from me! You pretended to love me!"

"I didn't pretend," he said with all apparent sincerity. Then he moved closer and put his hands on her arms. "Karrie. It was just that profits weren't coming as quickly as we'd hoped and while you were able to be patient about it, I'm a man of action." He smiled, as though considering that a revelation of good character. "I saw an opportunity to better my lot in life and I—"

He got no further. A fist shot out past Karen's shoulder. Brian remained standing for one moment of startled confusion, then he slumped to the ground, out for the count.

Charlie, wearing last night's suit, his white shirt open at the throat, caught the back of Brian's coat and dragged him to the curb. Then he took Karen's arm and walked her up the steps and into the house.

"Why were you even talking to him?" he asked.

She struggled desperately to get her bearings, to understand the weird disorientation Brian's appearance had caused in her. She'd once loved him. *Him.*

"Um..." While one part of her mind tried to deal with what this meant to her, another allowed her to explain to Charlie what Brian had wanted.

"He wanted you to put him up?" Charlie demanded in disbelief.

She nodded, looking into Charlie's eyes and thinking how much she loved him. But she'd once been sure she'd loved Brian.

The truth—the reality of her situation was beginning to come home to her. She'd known it in the beginning, but had allowed herself to forget so that she could have what she'd always wanted.

She smiled at Charlie sadly. "To his mind, it was in my best interest to help him. Can you believe I used to love him?"

Something tumultuous was going on inside her. He could feel the tension emanating from her, the stiffness in the shoulders under his arm. He wondered what else the creep had said to her.

He'd awakened twenty minutes ago with her all wrapped around him—but something had changed since then. He was sure it couldn't be that seeing Brian again made her realize she still loved him. He'd heard her shouting at him.

"What's going on?" he asked, trying to keep any suggestion of panic out of his voice.

"What do you mean?" Her wide, tired eyes were filled with phony innocence. "Come on into the kitchen. I was starting to get breakfast."

He caught her arm to stop her retreat. "Karen, come on. What is it? You can't still care for him?"

"Of course not."

"Then what's changed? Something has. Everything has. I can feel the difference."

Her pretense of innocence fell away and she looked suddenly miserable and sad. "I used to think I had nothing in common with Paula until last night when she told us how afraid she was of making mistakes. Well, so am I. But not because I've never made any, but because I make them all the time!"

"Everybody makes mistakes, Karen."

She nodded. "I can deal with not being very domestic and burning dinner, but I make the kind of mistakes that have life-changing consequences. Because I trusted Brian, my employees lost their jobs, my clients were in danger of losing their estimated tax payments. For the little guys that was a lot of money.''

Charlie was trying very hard to remember that she'd had a mostly sleepless night and a shock upon awakening that had probably jarred her usually sharp brain. "I understand all that. But you assumed responsibility for those things and took charge of the situation. There are other jobs for your employees, and you paid everybody's estimates out of your own pocket. Life's full of crises, but you weathered this one."

She looked at him as though they needed an interpreter. "Charlie. I loved Brian. I loved and believed in the man who cleaned out my bank accounts and came back to me the moment he was out of jail to ask me to give him a place to stay! How stupid is that?''

"So he was a better actor than you were a judge of character." He gripped her other arm also and gave her a small shake. "I just want to know that you're not thinking you could be making the same mistake with me."

She shook her head quickly. "No. It isn't you at all, it's... I just fell for this perfect little scenario and so did you. A reunion of high school dreamers. I mean, come on. What's wrong with us?"

Panic was now taking definite shape inside him. He forced himself to ignore it in order to think. "I wasn't aware there was anything wrong with us. What are you talking about? Have you ever had a better time than we have together?"

WHAT *WAS* SHE talking about? It was all kind of a formless fear swelling, billowing inside her so that she couldn't think. But portents of doom were being flung at her by the unseen hand of past experience. He wasn't for her. She wasn't for him. This couldn't be. It was too...too...perfect.

Okay, that didn't make sense. She had to stop thinking hysterically because he stood implacably beside her, waiting for her to make sense.

"I mean that it isn't real life," she said calmly, trying to sound philosophical.

He wasn't buying it. "What isn't?"

"You know." He still held her arms, so she flailed her hands in a gesture of helplessness. "A hometown reunion. Dreams coming true. Happily ever after. All that stuff."

"Dreams coming true," he said quietly, "is what life *is* all about. We pursue our dreams to make them our reality."

"Charlie." She struggled to maintain her point of view in the face of his seductive argument. "What has dreaming done for you? Put you in a job you ended up hating, in a marriage that dissolved, and in a tiny two-person family with your motherless son." She knew that was brutal, but she had to make him understand. "It put me in a relationship that destroyed my business and my belief in happily ever after."

He was silent for a moment, and she was just beginning to think he might be willing to concede when he replied. "Broken dreams are simply a matter of perspective. I left my job not because I hated it, but because what I saw made me more sensitive than I'd thought I was. And I didn't want to abandon that growth to continue."

He shifted in his seat, clearly as determined to

make her understand as she was to reach him. "And I don't think my marriage dissolved. The love was there, but Van and I were changing as people and it was hard to find that connection again. You know," he said. "The connection you and I have. Or that I thought we had. That sense that you're in harmony. Two different voices and one nicely blended sound."

His voice took on a little volume and suddenly, a little heat. "And Ben's and my two-person little family has given both of us a great deal of comfort and happiness. Unlike you, who has a life filled with wonderful if ditzy people, and all you garner from it is how inadequate they make you feel, or how demanding they are of you."

She stammered over a reply, and finally cried the generic, "You don't understand!"

"No, I don't," he admitted. "You came here to start all over. Your family..."

"I did not come to start over," she said firmly. There. She was reclaiming her original intent in coming to Bramble Bay. "This was a temporary measure."

"Oh, right," he said, a trace of scorn in his voice. "Well, when you live life in a temporary way, all you get from it is temporary stuff. Nothing takes."

"Brian was not temporary!" she said angrily, tears biting her throat and her eyes. "And look what happened! When you give it your all, you stand to lose it all, and I'm just not doing that again."

He studied her in silence until she began to fidget under his stare. "So I *am* that important to you," he said, as though just discovering that for a certainty. "And you understand that you're that important to me, but that doesn't fit the stop-gap style of living you've adopted to stay safe. Only wimps live that way, you know.''

"Fool me once, shame on you. Fool me twice—"

"Oh, don't quote that tripe to me," he interrupted. "You know I have no intention of cheating you or hurting you. You know I'm not Brian Spencer. I'm just Charlie. The guy who wanted to take you to the prom fourteen years ago because he was so impressed with your gutsy approach to everything." He opened his door. "But that's not you anymore, is it? You're the woman hiding behind the drapes in the four-poster bed. My mistake. 'Bye, Karen."

He closed the door with a slam and was gone.

CHAPTER NINE

THE DING OF THE Fasten Seatbelts sign invaded Karen's unconscious.

No. No, it couldn't be that. She wasn't on an airplane.

It was the sound of an elevator bell announcing its opening doors.

No. She was not on an elevator. Although she did feel a little as though she was in some sort of conveyance that had taken her below basement level. Things were dark and oppressive, almost suffocating. That was fine because she wanted to die anyway.

It was the sound heard on a hospital intercom just before a doctor was paged.

No.

Well, maybe. She did feel sick, and she was in a bed.

"My God, Karen! I've been ringing the doorbell for five minutes! What are you doing in bed at eleven-thirty? And get that pillow off your head before you smother!"

Hell. She was in hell. They must have elevators in hell to take you down, down, down to the deepest reaches of the inferno. Where her sister was opening the drapes, letting in the light, chirping at the top of her voice.

"Come on. We have a million things to do!

You're going to be my maid of honor, and we only have a week to find dresses. I know it's Sunday, but I brought a catalogue we can go through for ideas. Up, up! The furniture delivery truck was backing into the driveway when I let myself in, so hop to. Only in Bramble Bay do you get Sunday deliveries. I'll put on the kettle while you... Lord! Karen! What happened to you?''

That as Karen sat up and tried to make sense of all her sister's directives, to focus on her as she flitted around the room. She now stood in the doorway, apparently on her way out of the room, and was frozen in her tracks, her eyes wide and her mouth open in a shocked 'Ah!'

Karen remembered suddenly what *had* happened to her this morning and that she'd gone back to bed and cried herself to sleep. Her makeup was smudged, which seemed to be the reason for Paula's horrified expression.

The doorbell rang.

Hell. Lower Level.

Paula pointed to the bathroom. ''You shower and get dressed. I'll let the furniture guys in.''

''I THINK THE WING CHAIR should go by the fireplace.'' Paula studied it thoughtfully in its new cream-colored upholstery patterned with a subtle green-and-yellow stripe. It coordinated with the medallion-back settee now also wearing a new cream fabric covered in red, green, and yellow cabbage roses. The delivery men had just left and Paula insisted on helping Karen organize the room.

Karen had placed the chair at a right angle to the

sofa to give the end of the room closest to the kitchen a conversation area.

"Wing chairs always go near a fireplace," Paula insisted. "It's traditional. And sensible."

Karen picked up one side of the chair. "Then, by all means, let's move it. I wouldn't want my placement of the chair to thwart your sense of the traditional."

Paula came to pick up the other side and walked laboriously backward with it until they were near the fireplace. She put it down and studied Karen across it. "What did happen last night?"

Karen sighed. "We bailed you out of jail, remember?"

Paula pointed Karen to sit in the chair, then perched on the hearth bench at a right angle to her. "I meant the part of the night you spent at home."

Karen sat sideways to face Paula and drew her legs up, tucking her feet in their woolly socks under herself. "Too much," she said. "We made love. I can't stay here, Paula."

"What do you mean? Why not?"

"Because I'm beginning to think I just don't fit anywhere. When we were kids, I just never measured up to the rest of the family. So I moved away to the big city and did very well for myself, until I fell in love and made the biggest, stupidest mistake—"

"Ah, pardon me, but have you looked around at the rest of us? Do you think your mistake in any way makes you unique? Our parents are wonderful but screwy, our brother's a doll but oblivious, our sister-in-law...well, actually I'm starting to really like her now that we've gotten some of the starch out of her. And then there's me!"

Paula looked wonderful this morning, Karen thought. In snug black jeans and a short, fuzzy white sweater that highlighted the porcelain perfection of her skin, she looked reborn, renewed. And she was nauseatingly perky.

"I've been feeling so inadequate taking it out on Danny because loving him made me feel as though I had to be everything to him for the rest of my life and I wasn't sure I was up to it." She smiled with a sort of relaxed quality Karen had never seen in her before. "But Danny reminded me last night that though that was true, his job was to try to be everything to me. So we'd be supporting each other."

"He explained about Joanie?"

Paula waved that away as an issue. "I knew he wasn't fooling around with her. It was just something to use to put distance between us. That was easier than saying, 'I'm scared. I don't feel up to this.'"

"Good for you." Karen reached a hand out to her that she caught and held. "As your maid of honor I don't have to wear anything with ruffles and big bows, do I?"

Paula laughed. "No. I'm going to wear something chic with a hat—a suit or a dress, I'm not sure. You can wear whatever you want."

"I'm happy for you, Paula."

"Thank you. So am I." Paula sighed at Karen. "But what are we going to do about you? So, you were wrong about a man. He tricked you. It seems to me the fault was his."

Karen shook her head. "I just don't believe dreams come true like this, anymore."

Paula pinched her fingers and leaned toward her with a frown. "Karen, Charlie is not Brian. Are you sure you're not just being a little chickenhearted here?''

Though Karen angled her chin defensively, Paula dropped her hand and continued firmly. ''I mean, a dream come true isn't a finished product. It's only the opportunity to make of your life what you've always wanted. So, it's still up to you, and that's frightening.''

Karen opened her mouth to try to rebut that, but she couldn't. Paula might very well be right, she wasn't sure. She was afraid of so many things on so many levels, she couldn't quite separate and analyze everything one by one. It was much easier at this point, particularly remembering the disappointed look in Charlie's eyes this morning, to simply go in another direction.

Now that the living room and kitchen were repainted and the furniture reupholstered, she had only to buy new bedding for the rooms to complement her grandmother's collection of antiques. Then she might be able to hire someone, a couple perhaps, to run it for her while she explored other options. San Francisco or Los Angeles.

The doorbell rang, followed by a sharp rap on the door. Then the bell rang again persistently.

Karen and Paula looked at one another. ''Mom,'' they said simultaneously.

It *was* their mother, but her hair wasn't combed and she'd pulled on a raincoat over her nightgown. Something had compromised her usually unflappable demeanor.

Karen pulled her inside and Paula rose to help sit her in the wing chair. ''What's the matter?'' Karen demanded.

"Your father still isn't home," she said, on the brink of tears. "And neither is Peter. Becky's just beside herself. I guess they had a fight last night after the dance?"

Karen nodded. "At dinner. I was there."

"Well—" Adelle started to talk, then gasped in anguish, her mouth quivering. "I can't imagine what's happened. Maybe they met somewhere and took off together or maybe they had two separate accidents, or maybe Becky's right and they've both gotten tired of my complaints and her emotions and they've left us!" She delivered the last on a broken sob and burst into tears.

"I'll call Danny," Paula said, running to the phone.

Karen held her mother's hands and tried to calm her. "Where was Daddy going?" she asked. "Did you try the office?"

"I called all night long. But I knew he wouldn't go there. We had a fight about Jerry Walker and he left in a bad..."

"Becky's father?" Karen interrupted.

Adelle looked guilty as fresh tears contorted her face.

Wondering if she was on to something, Karen gently squeezed her mother's hands. "Mom, why would you and Daddy fight over Mr. Walker?"

Adelle sighed and seemed to try to pull herself together. "I went with him before I dated your father."

Karen stared, speechless for a moment. "You never told us that!" she gasped finally.

Her mother wrung an embroidered hanky in her

fingers. "Well, it's not a particularly sweet story. He asked me to marry him and I accepted, then…"

"Then?"

"Then Katie Simonsen came to tell me she was pregnant with his baby."

"You mean Katie that he's married to now? Mrs. Walker? Becky's mom?"

Adelle nodded. "Becky's oldest brother Chet was—premature."

The reason for her mother's antagonism toward Peter's wife was suddenly taking shape.

"That's why you don't like Becky?"

"I like Becky! I keep telling you that."

"But you pick on her."

Adelle wept, then sniffed and dabbed at her nose with the crumpled hanky. "Aren't I pathetic? It's just that I know how I am—opinionated, blunt, pushy. And I've always been like that. I was in medical school then and all the men I knew were afraid of me, but Jerry treated me like a princess. But apparently it didn't mean I was special, just that I was someone to be with while he was on the outs with Katie." She pushed at her hair. "I must look a fright."

"You look fine. So, what did you do?"

"I sent him back to Katie. I think it was a good decision. They've been happy."

Karen went to kneel beside her chair. "Have you been happy, Mom?"

"Of course, I have." She slanted Karen a wry smile. "I love your father. He treats me more like a buddy than a princess, but that's good, too. He didn't have the big ideas Jerry had, or the excitement over everything, but you soon realize in a marriage that that isn't what it's all about.''

"But, Mom. That sounds as though you've made peace with the situation. What is the problem with Becky?"

Adelle sighed and sat up straighter. "I'm not proud to admit it, but she looks just like her mother did in those days, and I remember so clearly how smug Katie was that she had her pregnancy to use against me." She shook her head. "I know how petty that is and I'm going to do better. Just, please, find your father and Peter!"

Karen stood, assimilating all this surprising information, and found Paula standing behind her, eyes wide, mouth agape. "Danny's got a couple of cars looking for them. What is...?"

"You try to relax, Mom," Karen said, taking Paula's hand. "I'll make some tea."

"But I..." Paula tried to resist, clearly wanting the part of the story she'd missed.

Karen yanked her forcefully, wishing Charlie was here to help her make sense of this.

CHARLIE FELT LIKE DEATH in a microwave—warmed over but cold in the middle. He was up and functioning but it was like an out-of-body experience, as though he was watching himself on a monitor, only visual input accepted. He had no thoughts, no feelings, and finally—no dreams.

He'd picked up Ben at the baby-sitter's and listened to his detailed recounting of watching *The Lion King* with her, of making popcorn, of taking a bubble bath and playing with a rubber duck.

"The bath stuff smelled girlie, though," Ben complained as they had breakfast at McDonald's. "But *The Lion King* was great!" He had his own copy and watched it several times a week. "And the duck was fun, but I like my Winnie-the-Pooh slide better. You can't splash as far with the duckie."

Charlie tried hard to push his depression aside and concentrate on his son. He'd seriously considered scuba gear for bath times. "I'm glad you had a good time."

Ben, perched on the edge of his seat, munched on his hash browns. "Did you have a good time at the dance?"

"Yes, I did."

"I bet Karen looked real pretty."

"That she did."

It hurt everywhere to even think that it was over just like that. But he could think of no solution short of coercion that would change anything.

"Are you gonna get married?"

"No." He wasn't sure how he was going to explain this to Ben, knowing how fond he'd become of Karen. He'd have to think of something later. He wasn't up to it this morning.

Ben, however, wanted information. "Not ever?"

"I don't think so."

"How come?"

"Because she doesn't want to be married right now."

"But I thought she liked us."

"She does. She likes you a whole lot." He struggled for words that would make sense to him. "But when two people get married, they have to want to do the same things."

"You mean like having tea together and stuff like that? She likes to do that with us."

"No, I mean like bigger stuff. Like wanting the same things out of life." That was getting him nowhere. "We really like living here and want to stay here. But Karen wants to go somewhere else eventually."

Ben's eyes grew wide with distress and he pushed away the rest of his breakfast. "You mean Karen's going away?"

"Not right away. But some day."

Ben swallowed, his eyes brimming. "And we'll never have tea with her again?"

Charlie packed up the rest of Ben's breakfast and handed him the toy that had come with it. "We'll just have to have tea with each other. Come on. Let's finish this at home and you can watch *The Lion King* again."

"I want to have tea with Karen!" Ben complained as they dropped their trash in the can and went out into the parking lot.

Yeah. So did he. He scooped Ben onto his hip and took him to the truck, trying to comfort him with promises of a fishing trip the following weekend.

Ben was not appeased.

Charlie pulled up in front of the factory and was shocked and a little concerned to find the shop door ajar. He hadn't been in the shop that morning, and when he'd left to pick up Ben, he'd walked out the door on the residence half of the building, which was around the side.

He wondered if the building had been broken into during the night, or if this was something that had happened since he'd left this morning.

He left Ben in the truck. "You stay right here, Ben," he said. "I'm going to check something out before we go into the house."

Charlie went to investigate, noting as he approached that the lock hadn't been broken or even tampered with. There was no sign of intrusion except a curious, low rumble coming from inside.

He braced himself as he pushed the door in soundlessly, wondering if he remembered any of the self-defense training he'd taken in his days as a reporter.

He walked into the room, only dimly lit by the watery daylight coming in through the windows, and saw no sign of theft or vandalism. Everything was as he'd left it yesterday afternoon to take Ben to the baby-sitter's and get ready for the dance.

He followed the strange sound to the far corner of the shop and bit off an expletive when he found the intruders fast asleep and snoring loudly on the old sofa and chair he kept for his own comfort when he worked late.

Ray Tillman was sprawled facedown on the sofa, one arm and one leg dangling off. Pete lay in the chair, his legs splayed out in front of him, his head tucked way down so that he could rest it on the arm. The area around them reeked of beer.

Charlie went to get Ben and brought him inside, putting *The Lion King* tape in the television/VCR he also kept in the shop so that he could have Ben nearby when he was busy.

"Why are Uncle Pete and Uncle Ray sleeping here?" Ben asked as Charlie fast-forwarded through the credits that always made Ben impatient.

"Just came to visit, I guess, and fell asleep waiting

for us. Here. You finish your breakfast while I see
what they want.''

"Dad?"

"Yeah?"

"Uncle Ray is Karen's dad, right?"

"Right."

"Well, maybe he could make her have tea with
us. You know. Like she doesn't get her allowance,
or her dessert or something.''

"Maybe. Watch your movie and I'll be back in a
few minutes.''

Ben nodded, already ensnared by the music.

Charlie struggled to pull a very limp Pete up in
the chair and shake him awake. He smelled like the
inside of the old Whale's Tail.

"Pete!'' Charlie shook Pete again as his eyelids
flickered. They opened widely, the hazel eyes beyond
them unfocused. "Pete, wake up! What are you doing here?''

"Um...key!'' Pete muttered, eyes closing again,
head slumping.

Charlie pulled him firmly upright and lightly
slapped his cheek. "I know how you got in,'' he said
as Pete's eyes flew open and blinked at him. They
had keys to each other's homes for undefined emer-
gencies. "But what are you doing here?''

"Drunk,'' Pete said, clearly trying hard to focus.
"Dad. Drunk.''

"Yeah, no kidding.'' Charlie leaned down as
Pete's chin began to sink. "But why? What happened? Do Becky and your mom know where you
are?''

Pete sneered. "Bachelors,'' he said with an idiotic
smile. "No more women. Just...babes.''

Amen, Charlie thought, then went to put on a pot of coffee. When he returned, Pete's eyes were open but staring sightlessly into a corner.

Ray sat in the middle of the sofa, his elbows on his knees, his head in both hands.

Charlie sat beside him. "What's going on, Ray?" he asked.

Ray winced and moved his hands to cover his ears.

It was from his vantage point on the sofa that Charlie noticed for the first time Pete's car through the window on the other side of the room. The blue-and-silver minivan sat in the empty parking lot of the pub across the street. He guessed it must have been there all night.

He didn't know what had happened and imagined it would still be a few minutes before his guests could tell him, but if these two had indeed been gone all night, he could just imagine what Adelle and Becky were going through.

Considering Becky's advanced pregnancy and an unwillingness to startle her, and the fact that he didn't know Adelle's number, he called Karen.

"Hello?" she said anxiously.

"Hi." His voice wasn't deliberately without expression, but at the sound of hers, he didn't think she'd want to hear what he felt. "Your dad and your brother are here," he said with little embellishment. "I don't know what happened, but they seem to have been trying to drink away some problem or other at Fogarty's and mercifully walked across the street to my place when they realized it wasn't safe to drive.

"I hadn't come into the shop this morning. I went to get Ben, then we went to breakfast, so I just found them. I'm sorry if your mom and Becky were worried."

"Mom's here," she replied, her voice, too, sounding stiff. He wondered if her reason for that was as good as his. "She's very upset. Paula's gone to see Becky. Thanks, Charlie. I'll come and get them."

"No, let me get some coffee down them and get them showered, then I'll drop them off. They smell like a lost weekend and look even worse."

"Okay. Charlie?"

"Yes?"

"Thank you." Her voice softened a fraction.

"Sure. See you in an hour or so."

Charlie plied Ray with coffee while Pete showered.

"Did you know that Adelle was once engaged to Pete's father-in-law?" Ray asked, his voice hoarse, his speech slow. At Charlie's frown of surprise, he went on. "She never had been able to forget him. She resents Becky because she looks like her mother, Katie, and she lost Jerry to Kate."

Charlie, sitting beside him, sipped at his own coffee. He was surprised to find he had energy for someone else's problems. "I didn't know that. But that doesn't necessarily mean that she still loves him."

Ray cast him a grim glance. "I tried to think about it that way, but it doesn't wash. So after we had this fight about it last night, I went to Fogarty's Pub to have a beer and think things through. Pete was already there."

Charlie took Ray's almost empty cup, went to the coffeepot to fill it up again, then brought it back to him. "I know he and Becky had a fight at dinner."

Ray nodded, then seemed to regret it, putting a hand to his forehead.

"Hang in there," Charlie said encouragingly. "You've got next go at the shower."

"I guess," Ray explained after a moment, "Pete and Becky fought more on the way home, Becky told Pete that if he couldn't be more sensitive to her needs and his family's, then she didn't think they had a future. So he dropped her home and kept going. To Fogarty's."

"Where the two of you plotted a trip to Vegas and a quest for babes?"

Ray raised an eyebrow. That gesture also seemed to hurt. He winced and rubbed his forehead. "How did you know?"

"Pete told me...sort of."

"Shower's all yours, Dad." Pete emerged from the residence in an old pair of Charlie's jeans and a gray sweatshirt. "Charlie left you a change of clothes on the foot of the bed."

Ray looked doubtfully at Charlie's lean proportions and his own paunchy middle.

"They're sweats," Charlie said as he went to pour Pete a cup of coffee.

Pete assumed his father's place on the sofa, then took a greedy sip of coffee. "Thanks, Charlie. I appreciate all the help."

"Sure. You realize you'll get murdered when you go home, anyway. Possibly even tortured first. I guess the ladies are very upset with the two of you."

Pete closed his eyes. "I don't know how things deteriorated to that degree. Are we the most dysfunctional bunch you ever saw, or what?"

"Actually, Paula's getting her life together thanks to the arrest."

Pete stopped, his mug halfway to his lips. "The what?"

Charlie explained about the middle-of-the-night call and Paula and Danny's conversation in the cell. "I'm not sure what the result was, but it sounded as though they were going to work it out when Karen and I left."

Pete took the sip, then leaned back and asked interestedly, "And how did you and Karen happen to be together at that hour?"

Charlie explained that, too—briefly.

Pete smiled. "So you're going to be my brother-in-law?"

Forced to concentrate on himself once again, Charlie felt the spurt of life in him that caring for his friends had caused, slow to a trickle. "No. She doesn't think this can be real."

Pete was confused. "How can anything be this bad and not be real?"

"Not you, Einstein. Us. And we're pretty good. But—I don't know. She has all this angst about living up to you and Paula, then all that stuff with Brian What's-his-name I guess makes it hard for her to trust me. He showed up at her house this morning."

"What? Isn't he in jail?"

Charlie told him what little he knew about Brian's appearance. "Seeing him reminded her that she sometimes doesn't do life very well—or so she thinks."

"Want me to talk to her?"

"No!" That came out more emphatically than Charlie had intended. "No," he said more reasonably. "She's got to work this out for herself, if she can. If she can't, then all I'm losing is what I didn't have before."

"That's a hell of a lot."

"Tell me about it."

The telephone rang and Pete shut his eyes tightly.

"Charlie, it's Karen!" Karen's voice said anxiously.

He felt a moment's alarm. "What? What's the matter?"

"Is Pete still there?"

"Yes, do you want to talk to—?"

"No! Tell him to meet us at the hospital. He's having a baby. When Paula got to his house, Becky's water had broken and she was already in labor. Mom and I are on our way."

"All right. We'll meet you there." Charlie hung up the phone. "You're having a baby!" he said to Pete as he went to get Ben and helped him pull on his jacket. "I'll drive."

Pete went to the door, then came back to the middle of the room, then headed back toward the door and collided with Charlie and Ben. He looked sober suddenly, but not entirely sane.

"Let's go, let's go!" he said, turning in a circle. "Where are my keys?"

"We're going in my car," Charlie reminded him. "You don't need your keys."

Ray walked out of the residence, pulling on the sleeves of the sweatshirt.

"Come on, Dad!" Pete shouted, pulling open the door. "Hurry up!"

"What—?" Ray began, even as he complied.

"The baby's coming," Charlie explained as they all headed out the door.

"I thought we had to get married to have a baby!" Ben said as he ran to keep up with the hurrying men.

"It's not our baby, it's Uncle Pete's." Charlie had to pull Pete out of the front of the truck in order to put Ben in the back.

"Oh." Ben lost interest and opened the book Charlie had thought to grab to keep him occupied.

Charlie pushed Pete back into the middle seat and helped Ray up beside him. He had to get friends with calmer lives, he thought as he sped toward the hospital.

CHAPTER TEN

"I WANT PETER!" Becky demanded, looking a little the worse for wear already after just half an hour at the hospital. Her hair was plastered to her forehead, her eyes filled with pain, and her disposition deteriorating. Her labor seemed to be progressing rapidly.

"He's on his way," Karen said for the tenth time. The elegant birthing room with its flower-sprigged wallpaper and homelike appointments was intended to create a cozy atmosphere, but almost seemed like the wrong setting for such distress. "Charlie's driving him and Dad."

Karen's reply was rapid breathing through a contraction and a groan of pain.

"Should she feel this bad this early?" Paula asked worriedly.

"This little guy's coming fast for a first baby." Adelle held Becky's hand and, in the absence of Peter, was coaching her breathing. "Happens sometimes. Peter was born a full half hour before Paula."

"I was probably enjoying my privacy." Paula winced as Becky cried out again. "Oh, geez! Even though I did an OB rotation, I'll never get used to this. I'm talking to Danny about adoption. I am not going through that for anybody."

Adelle shooed them toward the door. "You two wait outside. Send Peter in the minute he gets here."

"Wait!" Becky called. "Karen. I forgot my bag with a change of clothes and my warm socks. My feet are cold. Paula kind of rushed me. Could you...ah!...get it for meeee?" The question ended in another contraction.

"Right away!" Karen started for the reception area while Paula went in search of a cup of coffee for Adelle and ice for Becky.

Peter and her father and Charlie and Ben came through the revolving doors just as Karen headed for the parking lot.

"Peter!" she exclaimed. "She wants you. Room 211."

"How is she?" he asked, already walking backward toward the rooms.

"Okay, but needing your support. Hurry!"

"Where are *you* going?" Ray asked Karen as Peter hurried off.

"Becky forgot her bag with her change of clothes and things." She'd explained before she realized she had a few questions herself. "And where have *you* been?" she asked judiciously. "I thought only teenage boys stayed out all night drinking without telling anyone where they were going. Mom's beside herself. And a nice example to set your son, who is about to be a father."

Her father closed his eyes wearily. "That's nothing I haven't told myself. But it wasn't a deliberate plan of action. It just happened."

"You'd have never taken that as an excuse when I lived at home."

She noticed suddenly that he looked tired and in pain, and she wrapped her arms around him, regretting her hasty accusations. If her mother had driven her and her siblings and Becky around the bend, what must he have gone through?

"I'm sorry, Dad," she said hastily. "I know you've had a hard time, but Mom's been a mess while you were missing. She's just gotten herself together to help Becky. But now that Peter's here, you and Mom need to find a quiet corner and talk."

He bear-hugged her, then held her away to look into her eyes. "We're all here now, so quit worrying. Go get Becky's bag and hurry back." He kissed her cheek then headed in the direction of the rooms.

"Hi, Karen!" Ben reached both arms up for Karen's hug.

She felt her heartbeat accelerate as she stood face-to-face with Charlie. But let her gaze slide past his neutral expression as she gave his son a big squeeze. "How are you doing?" she asked. "Did you bring something to read?" She indicated the book he carried.

"Yeah. Somebody's getting a baby and we'll have to wait. You want to come with us?"

"The lady who's having the baby is like my sister, and she forgot something at home, so I promised to go get it for her. But I'll see you later, okay?"

"Okay. But I want us to have tea."

"When I come back," she promised, "we'll have tea in the cafeteria."

He looked puzzled. "What's that?"

"It's like a restaurant in the hospital." She gave him another hug, straightened up, and braced herself to look into Charlie's face.

"Thank you again," she said, "for looking out for Dad and Peter."

He nodded. "Well, they broke into my place, so I had little choice."

She shook her head over their behavior. "Bad genes, I guess."

He didn't say it, but she read in his eyes that she was part of that faulty pool. She pushed her way through the door and out to her car.

She retrieved Becky's bag then made a quick trip home, remembering that she hadn't fed Hannibal.

As she stepped inside and closed the door behind her, she was struck anew at how beautiful the rooms were in their new touches of paint and upholstery. They lent the beautiful old place a freshness that was both cheering and inviting.

And it might have worked its magic on her except that her eyes fell on the beautiful room divider Charlie had made as though he'd seen right into her thoughts and all she felt instead was the futility of all her efforts—and his.

Maybe she hadn't come home to start over. Maybe she'd only come here to run away from Seattle and memories of what Brian had done to her. Just as she'd run from here to Seattle so that if she failed, she could do so in private. Well, that had backfired big-time.

So, what now? Run again? She didn't want to. She wanted to stay with Charlie and Ben and her psychotic family more than anything, but it was hard to believe this could be the life for her. Perfection didn't happen to Karen Tillman.

Karen found Hannibal asleep on the kitchen floor in front of the cupboard where she kept the cat food. She stroked his back and he rolled over playfully, batting at her with his forepaws.

She picked him up and held him in one arm while she reached into the cupboard for a can of food.

He lay limply, now deeply in love with her and her regular meals and warm home. She could relate completely. Wasn't that what everybody wanted?

She scooped the contents of the can into Hannibal's bowl, gave him fresh water, and was washing her hands of the horrid giblets-and-kidney smell when the doorbell rang.

Drying her hands on a towel, she went to the door. A tall woman in a navy-blue suit and heels stood on the porch. Her sandy blond hair was caught back in an elegant twist, and her gray eyes looked Karen over with interest. Her face was vaguely familiar, but Karen experienced that feeling every time she walked down the street. Almost everyone in town was someone she'd once known, or related to, and similar in appearance to the people in her past.

"Good morning," Karen said, anxious to get back to the hospital. "Can I help you?"

The woman smiled and held her hands out at her sides, a small envelope clutch purse in one hand. "You don't remember me?"

Karen studied her more closely. "I was just thinking that you look very familiar. But I was away for some time and I—"

"Connie Powell!" the woman cried as though she couldn't wait another moment. "I'm Connie Powell. Well, Connie Pelligrino now. Harder to remember, but I didn't have to change my monograms!" She laughed at that as she wrapped Karen in a strong hug.

"Well, come in," Karen said, drawing her inside. Part of her was anxious to get back to Becky and the rest of the family, but she was also delighted to see her old friend. "I apologize if I seem distracted, but my sister-in-law is having a baby even as we speak. I just came home because she forgot something."

"How wonderful," Connie said. "We're in favor of babies at our house, too. Rick and I have three." She looked around her at the newly redecorated room. "What a beautiful place! Rick and I moved to Newport two years ago, but my stepmother is still here and she told me your mother told her that you're opening a B-and-B after the first of the year."

Karen nodded, leading her to the sofa. "Right. Sit, Connie. I thought I'd try my hand at something new. I'm sure you read in the paper about what happened to me."

Connie nodded grimly. "Aren't people just ruthless when they get a juicy tidbit? I wish I could have been more help to you when that happened, but I was having our third child." She gave Karen another spontaneous hug. "I'll never forget what you did for me in high school. My parents were very supportive about the pregnancy, but really—you spend so little time at home when you're that age between school and part-time work. I can't tell you what your support meant to me. And I wasn't trying to tell anyone that I was proud of my condition, or that I didn't wish things were different, I just wanted to be part of what was going on around me. I needed something to do to feel that I belonged somewhere and could contribute something."

"I'm so glad you've worked things out so well. Charlie Scott tells me you're a lawyer."

"I am. I went to Washington State and took the baby with me. I found a great day care that I paid for by helping out there when I wasn't in class. It was a very difficult couple of years, but we made it and I know I'm better for having done it all myself. You should see what a beautiful girl she's grown up to be. She's thirteen now.'' Connie smiled. ''Her name is Karen.''

Karen was unwilling to believe she was telling her she'd named the child for her.

''Yes. After you,'' Connie clarified. ''You stood up for me. You stuck your neck out on my behalf. You gave me value, so I was able to treat myself and my baby as though we were important.''

''Connie.'' Karen's eyes filled as Connie pulled a wallet out of her purse and pointed to a photo of a teenage girl. She had short blond hair with a dozen tiny butterfly clips in it, and her mother's eyes and smile. Karen. Her name was *Karen*.

''There she is. Isn't she beautiful? This is Lucy.'' She was a dark-haired little girl about seven. ''And this is one of those pictures they take in the hospital of our latest addition, Maggie.'' She flipped a few plastic sleeves and pointed to a wedding photo of herself and a stocky dark-haired man several inches shorter than she was, but who wore an expression that said he had stature if he didn't have height.

''This is Rick. He's the assistant D.A. in Newport. I have everything a woman could ever want, Karen, and I'm convinced that if it hadn't been for you, things might not have turned out this way for me.''

''Connie, you did this all yourself.''

''I did, but mostly because every time things got tough I could see you standing between me and Mrs. Perez, telling her that I deserved support not scorn and that if she didn't give it to me, you were going to the school board and the community. And then you did it!''

Karen stared at her. She'd known at the time that Connie was grateful for her support, but she'd never realized just how much it had meant to her.

''So, I was wondering. Since I was busy having a baby when you could have used my help, could I make up for that a little bit by booking the B-and-B for the last weekend in January?''

''Ah...sure.'' Business. Real business. Karen sat a little straighter, thinking she had no reservations book, no receipt book. And she had to get to the bank to arrange to accept credit cards. ''How many rooms did you want?''

''You have five?''

''Yes.''

''Then, all of them. My firm's doing a sort of R-and-R thing, and I thought it would be fun if we stayed here. I can send you details later if you can promise me you'll reserve these dates.'' She took a business card out of her purse and scribbled something on it, then handed it to her. Karen could tell by the suddenly intimate quality of her smile that they were about to change subjects. ''So, you're seeing Charlie Scott? I used to have a crush on him in high school like all the other girls did. It's nice to see that he matured with all the qualities you like to believe in in a man. He was sure tenacious about that little boy.''

She'd been about to deny that she was seeing Charlie, when Connie added that last sentence. Tenacious? ''I don't understand,'' she said frankly.

''The adoption,'' Connie clarified, or probably thought she did. All that word did was further con-

fuse Karen. "I moved heaven and earth to make sure
no father was going to come forward to claim the
baby. We finally found a reporter in Paris with *Le
Monde* who might have been, but who wasn't interested in claiming paternity and was happy to sign
away all rights to Ben."

Karen absorbed all that information in openmouthed astonishment.

"Oh, no." Connie put a hand to her mouth, then
dropped it to her lap. "You didn't know."

Karen blinked, unable to remember any suggestions in word or deed that Ben wasn't Charlie's natural child. "But his wife gave birth *eight* months
after she filed for divorce," she said.

Connie nodded. "But Charlie had been back home
a year when he got the call that she was dying. The
friend who called him presumed the baby was his—
but it wasn't. At least not biologically."

"My God," Karen whispered. "He's the most de-
voted father I've ever seen."

"I know. He said the moment he looked into the
baby's eyes, he felt a connection."

Karen remembered a conversation they'd had
about that. He'd seen so much death, that he'd wondered if he could ever have a normal life again. Then
he'd seen Ben and everything had changed. She'd
thought he'd meant because he'd known Ben was his
flesh and blood.

But he'd meant because he'd found this orphaned
child alone in the world, and opened his heart.

How could a woman *not* trust a man who could
do that?

"But I'm sorry. I guess I've said too much."

"You didn't. Don't worry." Now she really had

to get back to the hospital. She waved the business card in front of her. "Consider the place booked for you for these dates, and you let me know if you need anything else."

She stood and walked Connie to the door. Connie stopped on the porch to hug her again. "Take care, Karen. And when you see Charlie, tell him I'm sorry if he'd meant to keep it a secret. But if I knew that about a man, it would only make me love him more. So tonight…" she winked at Karen "…when you make extra-special love to him, he won't even know he owes me. 'Bye."

"'Bye. See you in January."

DAMON PETER TILLMAN looked like an angel and not at all the little devil his grandmother had feared. He weighed almost nine pounds, was very bald, and loudly screeched his displeasure at the cold, outside world. Then Becky, discreetly covering him and herself with the flowered blanket, gave him her breast.

"Huh!" Ben said loudly. "So that's what those are for." He never made embarrassing observations quietly.

Peter, Adelle, Paula and Ray laughed. The baby had been born half an hour ago, and Charlie and Ben had been invited into the room to admire him. Whatever animosity had been present among the two couples last night had been wiped away this morning by the baby's surprise arrival.

Peter sat on the bed, Becky and the baby propped against him. "What on earth's happened to Karen?" he asked, glancing up at the clock. "She's been gone over an hour. It shouldn't have taken her more than fifteen minutes to get Becky's bag."

Both her parents turned to the clock with concerned looks.

Charlie might have suspected her of avoiding him, but he knew she was excited about her nephew. "Why don't I find a pay phone," he suggested, "and call—"

He was interrupted as the door to the room burst open and Karen stood there, holding it open with her elbow. In her arms was a large, paper-wrapped bouquet of flowers and a three-foot blue plush moose with wide yellow antlers.

"Hi!" she exclaimed. Her eyes were bright, her face flushed, her hair all over the place.

"Karen!" her family cried in a unanimous expression of relief.

Charlie wondered if she had any idea how much they all loved and needed her.

She blew her bangs out of her eyes, smiled at everyone and approached the bed with a long, slow "Aaawww," filled with aunty love and adoration.

Ben tried to intercept her, used to always claiming her attention, but Charlie held him back. Ben stopped, but not happily.

"Damon!" she whispered as her parents relieved her of her gifts.

She got on her knees beside the bed and put a fingertip to the tiny hand resting on a plump cheek. Charlie felt Ben shift a little jealously.

"Oh, Becky," she said quietly. "Well done, girl. You, too, Peter. That is the prettiest baby I've ever seen." Then, with sweet sincerity, she turned to Ben. "Of course, I didn't see you when you were a baby. But I'm sure you were this beautiful."

Ben smiled brightly, his self-esteem restored.

"He was," Charlie assured her.

Then, with no warning or explanation, her dark eyes wandered over him like a sensuous touch, and that sweet smile she'd had for Ben was turned on him. His heart jolted against his ribs. What the hell did that mean?

Before he could figure it out, she turned back to the baby.

"Okay, give me the particulars," she asked of Becky and Peter. "Height, weight, etc."

Peter reeled them off.

"We were beginning to worry about you," Paula said. "What happened?"

"I stopped home to feed the cat," she explained, "and while I was there, an old friend stopped by and booked the B-and-B for an entire weekend, all five rooms."

"Great!" Peter said. "Who was that?"

"Remember Connie Powell?"

"Yeah. Married another lawyer, didn't she? Some guy from Denver. Somebody Palermo, or something?"

"Pelligrino."

"That's right. Well, good for you. Not even open yet, and you already have a full house for an entire weekend."

"When we call your grandmother tonight," Adelle said, "to tell her about Damon…" Everyone looked up at her correct pronunciation of the name. She went on as though she hadn't noticed. "We'll have to tell her what a success her house is already!"

Karen studied her smiling parents and asked carefully, "Sure. But…how are things on the home front with you two?"

Anyone else might have been embarrassed. But, Charlie reminded himself, these were the Tillmans.

"Good," Adelle replied. "Your father owes me something big and expensive for not killing him for last night, and everything else...is all straightened out."

Becky sent Peter a glare. "If I didn't love *you* so much, you'd be black and blue for last night."

He kissed her temple, looking contrite. "I'm sorry. You can beat me up as soon as you feel up to it."

The door pushed open once again and Danny walked in in uniform, holding a giant golden-brown teddy bear sporting a blue bow.

Paula ran to him, her face aglow.

"I can't stay," he apologized as Pete took the bear and shook Danny's hand. "I'm on a brief break. Just wanted to offer my congratulations."

"And ours to you!" Becky said. "I understand we're having a wedding before the christening."

"Finally," he said, giving Paula's shoulders a squeeze.

Paula blushed, delighting everyone.

Danny dutifully admired the baby, shook hands with Ray and hugged Adelle, then accepted Pete's and Charlie's congratulations and ruffled Ben's hair.

Paula walked him out of the hospital but returned shortly, a lingering smile on her lips.

Charlie listened patiently as the family made plans for the christening, then felt as though he had to leave the room or burst.

He loved the Tillmans like he loved his own family, and he was delighted by the safe arrival of their newest member.

But his personal future and his son's happiness

were on the line here and he couldn't stand around another second without telling Karen what he thought of her decision to cut them out of her life. And ask her how she could look at him like that after having done so.

He'd been drunk on their lovemaking and taken by surprise last night, but today he was thinking more clearly and he had a few arguments she was going to listen to. He wasn't going to let her kill what he felt without putting up one hell of a fight.

But he couldn't do it here and spoil this beautiful family moment. It had to wait until later. It might kill him in the meantime, but it would have to wait.

He began to excuse himself and Ben when Karen got to her feet and said with a polite smile in his direction, "But I promised to take Ben to tea in the cafeteria." She put her hand out and Ben went right to her and caught it, abandoning him as though he'd never seen him before in his life.

"Charlie, are you coming?" Karen asked.

"No," he said. He heard the communal indrawn breath of their companions. "I mean I'd like to talk to you first," he qualified. He leaned down to put his hands on Ben's shoulders. "I'm sorry, buddy. I know you've been anxious to have tea, but I have to talk to Karen for a few minutes first, okay? Can you stay with Paula until I come and get you when we're finished?"

Ben looked uncertainly from Charlie to Karen. Paula drew him onto her lap and reached for the book he'd left on the end of the bed. "How about if I read to you? I see you brought a great book."

"You won't yell at her," Ben asked him, "and make her go away, will you?"

Everyone waited with interest for his answer.

"I might yell at her," he said. He never lied to Ben. "But I won't let her go away. We'll be back for you in a few minutes."

"Okay," Ben said finally, then turned to Paula and took the book from her. "I'll read it to *you*," he said.

Charlie led Karen into the corridor, then looked right and left for somewhere private to talk. The waiting area at the end was crowded with people, so he led her outside into a rare, sunny afternoon.

KAREN NOTICED that the air was rich with the salt and diesel smells of Bramble Bay, and the fragrance of woodsmoke and something baking somewhere. The sun had made a rare appearance, and the russet and gold of oak and vine maple against a cloudy blue sky was heartbreakingly beautiful.

She thought it odd that she should notice that when she knew that her happiness hung by a thread. Charlie did not appear to be in a forgiving mood, and she had no idea how to explain to him that just this morning she'd been sure she was incapable of being what he and Ben needed for a lifetime, yet now, thanks to a reminder of the scrappy young woman she'd been, it seemed doable.

Love, she realized, had turned up the power on her senses.

Even as Charlie walked her around the corner from the hospital's main entrance and backed her against the side wall, one arm braced against it to hold her there, she saw silver and gold shards in the depths of his blue eyes, noticed the breeze catching and swirling the dark hair at his forehead, heard the anger in his voice and still loved the sound of it.

"What's going on?" he asked.

Okay. She needed one more minute to collect her courage. "Going on?" she stalled.

"That look you gave me in Becky's room. What is going on?" He separated the last four words for emphasis.

Okay. This was sink or swim, do or die, the old brave Karen or the 'fraidy one.

"Discovery is going on," she replied, trying to imbue her voice with confidence. She didn't feel it, but she wanted him to think she did. "Enlightenment. A veritable epiphany!"

He made a production of looking at his watch. Then he looked at her, and whatever hope she'd entertained that this might be easier than she'd hoped went out the window. "Six hours ago, you were convinced that you and I were living in a soap opera or the pages of a book. 'This isn't real,' I think you said."

She nodded. "I know. I was wrong."

"I tried to tell you that," he pointed out. "But you didn't believe me."

"I had to find out for myself."

"And how did you do that? What brought about this epiphany?"

"Connie Powell," she replied.

She saw the suspicion form in his eyes and the anger deepen there. She leapt quickly to Connie's defense. "Yes, she told me about Ben, but it wasn't her fault. She just started talking as though I knew about the adoption." Then she tried to shift a little blame on him. "I guess because she knew we were seeing each other, she thought you might have told me."

He sloughed it off. "That's a confidence for people in love. And when would I have done that between the time you told me you loved me, promptly fell asleep in my arms, hauled me off to bail your sister out of jail, then told me the first moment we had a little privacy that I wasn't real and we had no future?"

"Fine," she conceded. "You get that one."

He dropped his arm, put both hands in his pockets and leaned back against the wall. "Frankly," he said with a disarming shrug, "I often forget that he isn't mine by birth. The first time I saw him, we looked each other in the eye, recognized kindred, lonely spirits, and forged a bond."

He spoke those words gently, his eyes unfocused. Then his gaze settled on her and he was grave again. "But why should that affect how you feel about me? I couldn't abandon a helpless infant whose mother had just died and whose father was nowhere to be found. I'm sure many people would have felt the same way."

"Not many men," she argued.

"It was simple compassion."

"It was openhearted generosity," she corrected. "It was that step out in faith so few of us are ever able to take."

He moved away from the wall, then turned back to confront her with a frown. "That doesn't prove anything to you about my potential as a husband. About me as a man you could love."

She blinked at him. "Excuse me. It tells me everything. I don't know what standard men use to judge women, but a woman looks for someone she can hand her heart to—the lovely, loving part and the ugly, selfish part—and trust him not to hurt her or shame her with it. Or steal it and all her stuff.''

He looked as though he was trying to understand, but couldn't quite. ''All right,'' he said, his voice softening just a little. ''But what I don't like about this is that you knew me before. Have I done anything since you've been home to suggest I'd ever hurt you in any way?''

''No, you didn't,'' she admitted, ''but I'd just been very hurt and you were right when you said I was hiding in my curtained bed. But it wasn't just that I didn't trust you. I wasn't sure I could trust myself, either.''

''To do what?''

''To love you as you and Ben deserve. To be for you all the things I'd want you to be for me.''

''But I never questioned that about you.''

''Yes, and that made it worse. You considered me something I wasn't. Or something I used to be but wasn't any longer. That was something else you said this morning.''

He sighed and nodded. ''I was angry this morning. And very, very disappointed. I thought we finally had the dream.''

She took a step forward and put her hand to his chest. He didn't stop her, but he didn't touch her, either.

Still, she felt his warmth and his heartbeat and they energized her.

''Paula told me dreams that come true are just a work in progress. They're not the final product, just an opportunity to work on it. And I think that's what I was afraid of. Here we were, coming together so beautifully just as I'd dreamed all those years ago, but I'd just made a horrible mistake with Brian, and though I never mistook you for him, I knew I was the same woman who'd made that mistake. What if I couldn't come through for you?''

''I never once,'' he said emphatically, ''considered that could happen.''

''Good.'' She drew a deep breath. Now she had to make her case. ''It was simple fear,'' she said. ''Then Connie reminded me of the person I used to be before my paranoia about measuring up to my family and the fear of making mistakes took over. And I realized as I was driving here that maybe it isn't as important to be right or to be smart as it is to just be *there*. To show up to do your part. Because it isn't ever about how it looks to anybody else, anyway, is it? It's about what we are to us, to each other. To Ben.''

For one agonizing moment he stared at her without speaking. Then she saw in his eyes the instant he understood and believed her.

He wrapped his arms around her and crushed her to him. ''You scared the hell out of me!'' he scolded gruffly.

''When you left this morning,'' she whispered for lack of air, ''I wanted to die. I thought I wanted freedom from the responsibility of loving someone, but when I had it, it felt like I was in Paula's tiny jail cell. And I was all alone in it.''

He tugged on a handful of her hair until he could look into her eyes. ''Now do you believe we're real?'' he asked.

''I do,'' she replied.

''That we're a dream come true?''

''I do.''

"That we'll love Ben together, and we'll love our families and do our best to endure with them whatever agonies they inflict upon themselves."

"I do."

He smiled into her eyes, his filled with love and desire, and she thought she might die of happiness.

"And when Pastor Cox says, 'Do you take this man?' your answer will be?"

She laughed softly, thinking how happy she was to be home. "I do," she said.

Your Romantic Books—find them at

www.eHarlequin.com

Visit the *Author's Alcove*

➢ Find the most complete information anywhere on your favorite author.

➢ Try your hand in the Writing Round Robin— contribute a chapter to an online book in the making.

Enter the *Reading Room*

➢ Experience an interactive novel—help determine the fate of a story being created now by one of your favorite authors.

➢ Join one of our reading groups and discuss your favorite book.

Drop into *Shop eHarlequin*

➢ Find the latest releases—read an excerpt or write a review for this month's Harlequin top sellers.

➢ Try out our amazing search feature—tell us your favorite theme, setting or time period and we'll find a book that's perfect for you.

All this and more available at

www.eHarlequin.com
on Women.com Networks

HARLEQUIN®
Makes any time special ™

HARLEQUIN® *Presents~*

Meet sophisticated men of the world and captivating women in glamorous, international settings. Seduction and passion guaranteed.

Sexy, fast-paced stories that reflect the attitudes, desires, lives and language of women today.

HARLEQUIN®
Temptation.

Vivid historical romances that capture the imagination with their richness, passion and adventure.

Harlequin®
® *Historical*

HARLEQUIN®
I N T R I G U E®

Electrifying romance and heart-stopping suspense that make for an exhilarating read.

Harlequin Romance®

Love stories that capture the essential dream of pure romance.

HARLEQUIN
Duets.

A fun, entertaining "lighter side of love" read that delivers romance with comedy.

Romance is just one click away!

online book serials

➤ *Exclusive* to our web site, get caught up in both the daily and weekly online installments of new romance stories.

➤ Try the Writing Round Robin. Contribute a chapter to a story created by our members. Plus, winners will get prizes.

romantic travel

➤ Want to know where the best place to kiss in New York City is, or which restaurant in Los Angeles is the most romantic? Check out our Romantic Hot Spots for the scoop.

➤ Share your travel tips and stories with us on the romantic travel message boards.

romantic reading library

➤ Relax as you read our collection of Romantic Poetry.

➤ Take a peek at the Top 10 Most Romantic Lines!

Visit us online at

www.eHarlequin.com

on Women.com Networks